D1245730

ARDED

0135702315

THE EARL'S
SNOW-KISSED
PROPOSAL

Alongside the Christmas-tinged atmosphere he became aware of the attention and buzz directed at him, on his first public appearance for nearly a year. It came as almost a relief as his body and mind spun automatically into action. Time to walk the walk and talk the talk. It was crucial to ensure that the press didn't work out why he was really here this evening, and that meant he must speak to all and sundry so that no one would identify his real quarry.

A smile on his lips, he headed towards his host and hostess—they should be able to point him in the right direction.

Etta Mason stepped behind an enormous potted plant and hauled in breath so hard her lungs protested as she checked her mobile phone for the gazillionth time.

This had been a mistake of supersonic proportions. *Breathe, Etta.* It would be OK. Cathy was safe. Images of her beautiful, precious sixteen-year-old daughter streamed through her mind. From babyhood to teenagedom she'd loved and looked after Cathy—sure, it had been hard sometimes, but not once had she regretted the choice her sixteen-year-old self had made. Whatever it had cost her.

Safe. Cathy is safe.

She was at a sleepover with her best friend, and most crucially of all there was no way that Tommy could find her. Etta dug her nails into the palm of her hand. Cathy had managed without her father thus far and that was how it would stay.

Determination hardened inside her. She had the situation under control. So now she needed to get on with her job. This was an important event and she had promised Ruby Caversham that she would do a pre-dinner talk. Therefore skulking behind potted plants was really *not* on the agenda. Instead she would step out in her pink-and-white candy cane dress and… And walk crash-bang into a very broad chest.

'I am *so* sorry. Put it down to a combination of high heels and innate clumsiness… Thank goodness I didn't impale y—'

The words died on her lips as she took in the appearance of the man she had nearly spiked with her candyfloss-pink heels. Short dark blond hair, blue-grey eyes that caught the light from the wall-mounted candles and cast a strange spell on her, a firm mouth that her gaze wanted to snag upon—especially when a smile tipped it up at the corners…

Etta blinked. *Holy moly!* There could be no

gainsaying that this man had charisma. *Whoa...* Her brain cells finally caught up and she stopped gawping as recognition sent out a flare. The man in front of her was none other than Gabriel Derwent, Earl of Wycliffe, heir to the Duke of Fairfax.

Great! The first time she'd been poleaxed by a man since...since *never*, and it turned out to be a man she despised. True, she didn't actually *know* him—but what kind of historian wouldn't follow the exploits of a leading member of the aristocracy? A man whose ancestors had been instrumental in the most gripping moments of English history.

In fairness, she had no issue with the playboy lifestyle he'd enjoyed for years—it was his more recent actions that had left her enraged. Nine months ago Gabriel Derwent had renounced his playboy way of life, wooed Lady Isobel Petersen, wined her and dined her and taken her to visit his parents—all of it recorded in celebrity magazines worldwide. He had even been papped in a jewellery store, scanning the engagement rings, and then...*kabam*! On the verge of a proposal Gabriel Derwent had unceremoniously dumped Lady Isobel and fled the country.

There had been a short but excited media outburst before the efficient Derwent publicity machine had rolled in, and Etta had taken the plight of Lady Isobel to heart. Etta *knew* how it felt to be deceived, to become enmeshed in a situation only to have it exposed as an illusion, and she could almost taste Lady Isobel's bitter hurt. A hurt inflicted by *this* man.

Her eyes narrowed as she returned his gaze.

His blue-grey eyes studied her face as he held out a hand, and something sparked in their depths. 'I'm Gabriel Derwent.'

For an instant her gaze snagged on his hand. Capable, strong, thick-fingered…and suspended in mid-air. *Get with it, Etta.* The last thing she wanted was for Gabriel Derwent to believe her to be flustered by his presence.

Clasping his hand in a brief handshake, she mustered a cool smile. 'Etta Mason.' She ignored the surely imaginary lingering sensation from his touch.

'Etta Mason…eminent historian.'

The words were more statement than question, and for a daft second she wondered if he had been lurking by the potted plant waiting for her. How ridiculous was that?

'That's me.'

For a moment she recalled the sheer struggle it had been to obtain her qualifications: the constant exhaustion as she'd strived to combine being the best mum she could be with the hours needed for study and working part-time. So no way would she go for false modesty—she *was* one of the best in her field.

As his eyes swept over her appearance she clocked a hint of surprise and ire sparked. Presumably her outfit didn't match up with his idea of 'eminent historian'.

'You look surprised?'

There was a pause as he contemplated his answer, and then he lifted his hands in a gesture of surrender. 'Busted. I'll admit that my preconceived idea of a renowned historian didn't include a bright-pink-striped dress. But I apologise unreservedly. I shouldn't have made such a stereotypical assumption. So how about we start again? I'll forget you nearly impaled me with your shoes and you forget my stupidity? Deal?'

This was her cue to close this conversation down—make a light comment and then walk away. But the relaxed tilt of his lips vied with the determined glint in his eye. Gabriel Derwent was turning on the charm—and Etta wanted to know why. She certainly didn't qualify as his type. Gabriel Derwent had been linked with a fair few women—all beautiful, all famous and all shallow—and none of them serious until the Lady Isobel Petersen debacle. So why would he show an interest in *her*?

The idea was laughable—Gabriel Derwent and a historian. And not just any old historian but one who had been a single mother at seventeen. True, he didn't know that, but Etta knew the ballroom held plenty of women more suited to be the recipient of the dazzling Derwent smile. It could be that she was overanalysing, and that he charmed on automatic, but instinct told her otherwise and curiosity tickled her vocal cords.

'Deal.' There could be no harm in a conversation, right? 'So how do we do that?'

'How about you tell me a bit about yourself? A day in the life of a prominent historian?'

His interest seemed genuine, even if she didn't get it. 'Part of the reason I love what I do is that all my days are different. I recently helped an author research a historical novel. I investigate family trees...help organise historic events. I blog for a historic society, I've written articles, I've done guest lectures...'

'Ruby told me you were one of the most committed professionals she knew.'

'Well, I feel the same about Ruby. And Ethan. What they do for the kids their foundation helps is inspiring. I wish—' Etta broke off. Her admiration for Ruby and Ethan Caversham and the ways in which they sought to help troubled teens—kids in care or on the street—stemmed from personal experience. How she wished she'd been able to turn to people like the Cavershams in her own time of need. But that was not a wish she had any inclination to share.

'What do you wish?'

Surprise touched her at the hint of perception in his voice—almost as if he too could empathise with the children out there who needed help—and for an instant an absurd flicker of warmth ignited her. *Ridiculous.* Gabriel Derwent had come into the world housed and shod, with a whole drawer full of silver spoons to choose from.

'I wish I did as much good as they do,' she improvised. After all it might not have been what she'd meant to say but it was the truth.

'Ruby mentioned that you'd done some work for her?'

The words niggled Etta. Ruby always had a good word to say about others, but that almost sounded as if Gabriel Derwent had expressed a specific interest in Etta. *Could* he be interested in her?

To her irritation the idea set off a spark of appreciation, caused her gaze to snag on his firm mouth, sent a strange, long-forgotten tingle down to her toes. Jeez, she must be losing it big-time— the idea was nuts.

Focus on the conversation, Etta.

'I did. From time to time she deals with children who only have a name for their birth parent and want to know more about them.'

'So you're almost playing detective?'

'Yes—that's what's so fascinating.' Though that fascination held an element of the bittersweet— a reminder that all her research and effort hadn't unearthed a single clue as to the identity of her *own* birth parents.

A familiar ache kicked at her ribcage and she clenched her nails into her palms. *Enough. Accept it.* She would never know who they were or why they had abandoned her on a doorstep thirty-two years ago. *Move on.*

'What if you discover something people don't want to hear?' Now darkness edged his voice, and matched the shadow in his grey-blue eyes.

'I tell them anyway. It's better to know.' This she knew. After all, *her* adoptive parents had hidden the truth of her birth from her—hadn't even told her she *was* adopted. Instead they had woven a web of illusion around her life—a mirage that had been exposed when they'd had a child of their own and turned Etta out into the cold.

Enough. Accept it. Move on.

Aware that his grey-blue eyes were studying her expression with a penetration she wouldn't have believed a man of his reputation capable of, she summoned a smile. Hoped to combat the fervour her voice had held. Somehow their conversation had taken on way too much depth—and, worse, she had no idea how or why that had happened.

'After all, they say knowledge is power.'

'So they do.' Now his voice matched her lightness, and suddenly there was that smile again. Full of charm. And she wondered if she had imagined the whole other side to the conversation.

'And sometimes knowledge is just useful. I did one job for Ruby when a pregnant teenager in care wanted to find out her medical history.'

It had been a case Etta had related to all too well. How many times had she looked at Cathy and worried that genes she knew nothing about might have an adverse medical impact on her daughter?

'Although the other side to *that* coin is the fact that in the past no one understood genes and everyone got on with it. Sometimes I believe we have to make a leap of faith,' she said.

'And just believe in fate?'

So now they had plunged into philosophical waters. 'Sometimes. Don't you agree?'

A flare burned in the depths of his eyes. 'No, I don't. We choose our fate because we have the power of choice.'

The intensity of his voice prickled her skin.

Then his broad shoulders lifted in a shrug. 'Or at least that's what I choose to believe.'

Enough. The Earl of Wycliffe possessed more depth than she'd given him credit for, but that didn't alter anything. The man was at best a playboy and at worst a heartbreaking master of illusion. Etta still had no idea why he'd engaged her in conversation for so long but it didn't matter. So...

'It's nearly time for my talk and I really must mingle. Hopefully the more people I talk to the more people will enjoy my speech. I'll say goodbye.'

'I look forward to your talk and to chatting again afterwards.'

Really? This didn't make sense. Curiosity surfaced and she pushed it, her besetting sin, down ruthlessly. There were way bigger items on her plate right now.

Etta summoned up her coolest smile. 'I won't

be staying long tonight, so in case we don't get a chance to speak again I'll say goodbye now.'

'And I'll say goodbye for now,' he murmured, so softly that she couldn't be sure she'd heard him correctly.

CHAPTER TWO

GABE WATCHED FROM a corner of the beautifully decorated ballroom as Etta Mason headed towards the podium with a sinuous grace. *Damn.* There it was again. The tap of attraction that had sparked when she'd first emerged from behind the potted plant earlier—a complication he hadn't anticipated.

In recent months his libido had been in hibernation mode. Plus the photo on her website hadn't prepared him for Etta Mason in the flesh, and the instant impact had caught him unawares. In real life her brown eyes were flecked with hints of amber and her generous mouth called for his attention. Glossy chestnut hair seemed to invite the touch of his fingers, and the slant of her cheekbones would cause envy in the heart of many a supermodel. But it wasn't only her beauty that had stopped him in his tracks—her expression had held a piquancy, a poise, that summoned notice.

Right now he needed to derail that train of

thought and pull his libido under control. He required Etta Mason's *professional* expertise. Urgently. So this attraction needed to be sidelined.

Etta tapped the microphone and waited for silence, showing no sign of nerves as she waited for the hum of chatter to die down. She stood with poise and stillness, her sleeveless pink-and-white-striped dress emphasised the slenderness of her waist and the soft material of its skirt artfully swathed over the curve of her hips and fell to her ankles in sleek, diaphanous curves.

Her expression held calm, her tawny brown eyes looked directly out into the audience, and her lips curved upwards in a relaxed smile. The only small indication of tension was the way she tucked one short tendril of brown hair behind her ear.

'Ladies and gentlemen…I promise not to keep you for long. But before I begin I want you all to think about something that I feel is a staggering fact. Every single one of us here had an ancestor alive in medieval times, in Tudor times, in Victorian times.'

Gabe could almost hear the sizzle as the attention of the audience was caught.

'Some of us—' Did her gaze linger on him for a second? '—may have had ancestors who stood in this very room and feasted with kings. For others those ancestors might have been common soldiers or ale-keepers, stonemasons or cutpurses or highwaymen. We all have family trees, and all trees need roots. Tonight I want to think about what those roots mean to us. As you know this ball is a fundraiser for teenage kids who have had a pretty tough start in life for one reason or another. Many of those children say they feel rootless, or uprooted…'

As she spoke her voice vibrated with passion. She cared—*really* cared about her subject, and about these kids. It was something he recognised and respected in Etta Mason, in the Cavershams and in himself. An empathy that drove him to work with children who were victims of bullying and with the bullies themselves, to carry out charity work that he had not and *would* not make public.

It was not relevant to the here and now. And yet Etta's genuine concern was an additional point in her favour as her speech came across as heartfelt but delivered with a professional edge.

A sweep of her hand indicated her dress. 'I chose to wear this because it reminds me of Christmas and the traditional candy canes. Christmas is a time full of traditions—a time when families get together. As such, it is a difficult time of year for a lot of children in care and a lot of children who *should be* in care. The money raised today will help kids like those enjoy a better Christmas and help them towards a future in which they can hopefully put down some new roots of their own. So when it comes to the auction please dig deep, in the spirit of Christmas. Enjoy the rest of your evening, and thanks for listening.'

As applause broke out Gabe stepped forward. Decision made—he'd come here to assess whether Etta Mason could do what he needed and now he knew for sure. So he'd shut down the feeling of attraction and start on the mission he'd set himself.

A few purposeful strides and he'd cut through the people who clustered around her. As he reached her side, surprise sparked in the exotic brown of her eyes.

'Impressive speech.'

'Thank you.'

'I was wondering if I could have a word in private. We could stroll on the terrace before we eat.'

For a second he thought she'd refuse, in which case he'd fall back on his reserve plan, but after a fractional hesitation she nodded.

Five minutes later they stepped out into the clean, cold air and Etta gave a small gasp that undoubtedly denoted appreciation. 'It's beautiful!'

Potted greenery twinkled with fairy lights and lanterns hung over the tables dotted about the mo-saic-paved terrace, casting a warm, magical glow whilst outdoor heaters combated the chill of the night air.

'The Cavershams know how to throw a party. There's outdoor dancing planned for later. It's a shame you have to leave early.'

A sudden image of Etta Mason in his arms as they glided round the moonlit mosaic tiles pierced his brain with a strength that sent a tingle through his body. Without thought his feet carried him a step closer to her, and a tantalising overtone of her vanilla scent teased his senses.

'Yes, it is.'

For a heartbeat he wondered if her mind had followed the same path as her brown gaze held his and flared with an intensity that caught his breath. Then the instant was over.

Her lips thinned and she muttered a *'tcha'* under her breath before moving away from him towards the wooden railings that surrounded the terrace. Once there, she turned to face him, arms folded. 'Why did you bring me out here?'

Her voice was tinged with suspicion—and who could blame her? Self-irritation coursed through his veins. He needed this woman in a professional capacity, and this conversation was way too important to risk it for the sake of a flare of thoroughly *unprofessional* attraction. Time to get back on track.

'I need a historian and you fit the bill.'

Surprise creased her brow as she assessed his words. 'Tell me more.'

Gabe kept his pose relaxed, indicating one of the wooden tables overhung with delicate white lit-up stars suspended from the glittering arbour. 'Shall we sit?'

'Sure.' Etta walked over and lowered herself into the chair with a wary grace.

Gabe followed suit, taking the opportunity to marshal his thoughts and line his words up like troops.

'I'd like you to put together a detailed family tree of the Derwent family, going back centuries. About eighteen months ago a much-publicised flood hit Derwent Manor and a lot of valuable items were destroyed—including a parchment that documented the basic Derwent family tree. A lot of the supporting documentation—ledgers that date back centuries—were also damaged and muddled up. Unfortunately I've now discovered that those records were never computerised. I'm sure some of the facts are a matter of public record but I wouldn't have the first clue how to access them let alone piece them all together.'

She leant forward, those amber-flecked eyes sparking with interest now, and for a perverse moment he felt chagrin that they hadn't been ignited by *him*.

'So you want me to put your family tree back together?'

'Yes. But in way more detail than the original.'

For centuries the dukedom had passed from father to son, and now that would come to an end. Which meant he needed to clamber up the family tree, delve down obscure branches and work out who might succeed to the dukedom after him, now that he knew he would never have a son of his own.

Frustration coated his insides. It was imperative that he understood his options—and fast. His father's recent heart attack meant the Duke and Duchess wanted him, the heir, to marry and produce a son at speed. That couldn't happen. But Gabe had no wish to trigger another heart attack in his father and the enormity of learning the truth might well do exactly that. So he had to come up with a strategy…a way to deal with it.

'There is another stipulation. I need it done by Christmas. I realise that this is a big job to ac-

complish in only a few weeks, but I'll do everything I can to help. As you may know my father
recently suffered a heart attack. I'd like to present him with the family tree as a surprise gift.'

The animation left her face and she shook her
head. 'I'm sorry. I have family commitments—
I'm leaving the country in a couple of days on a
five-week holiday.'

Disappointment weighed upon him. He'd done
his research and Etta had seemed the perfect can-
didate. Now he'd met her, every instinct told him
she would do the job right and fast. 'Any chance
you'd postpone? I'd amply compensate you and
you can name your fee.'

'It isn't about money. I'm taking my daughter
on a cruise.'

Daughter. Somehow it hadn't crossed his mind
that Etta might have a daughter—there had been
no mention of a husband or children on her website—and for a second the idea of their existence
twanged a chord of disappointment inside him.
No. The whole attraction thing had been closed
down. But on a professional level he wanted Etta
Mason for the job. So…

'You're sure? Perhaps your husband could take
your daughter and I'd pay for another family
holiday.'

'There is no husband. Thank you for the opportunity, but I really can't accept the job.'

Now her words held regret, and a shadow that betokened disappointment clouded the amber of her eyes. Gabe frowned. Maybe he could change her mind—cruise or no cruise, he sensed she wanted the job. Time to utilise his reserve plan.

As if on cue the dinner gong pealed out and he rose to his feet. 'We'd better go in.'

Etta swallowed down a sigh. To trace the Derwent family tree ranked up there with her ideal job. Gabriel Derwent had offered her the opportunity to access papers and records of the past, to piece together a lineage that stretched back over centuries and complete a jigsaw puzzle of historical import, to lose herself in the life of people who had existed in times gone by.

On top of that a high-profile case like this would have boosted her reputation and it would have paid well. Nothing to sneeze at if ousting Tommy from her life ever involved a need for legal aid.

Tommy. Fear shivered through Etta—she would *not* let Tommy become part of their lives again. Nothing could compare with the importance of removing Cathy from Tommy's orbit. So this golden opportunity would have to be passed by.

Yet disappointment twinged, compounded by an inexplicable feeling of chagrin that he looked so calm. Which was further complicated by a memory of that moment on the terrace—that heartbeat of time when she had been aware of him with an intensity that had rocked her senses.

So all in all it was a relief to re-enter the warmth and grandeur of the hotel and join the throng of guests headed for the banqueting hall.

Once there, Etta stopped on the threshold. 'I'd better go and find my place.'

'I can help you there. You're at Table Five. Same as me.'

Etta frowned. 'No. I checked the seating plan earlier.'

'There's been a slight change to the plan.'

A flare of anger heated her veins at his sheer arrogance and she spun to face him—she would *not* be manipulated. 'Are you telling me *you* altered it? Ruby puts a huge amount of thought into these arrangements—you can't change them to suit yourself.'

'Relax, Etta. I asked Ruby if she would change it. You told me you had to leave early, and I wanted to make sure I got the chance to speak with you about the job.'

That made sense, and yet alarm bells began to

clang in her head. She narrowed her eyes with suspicion. Gabriel Derwent was used to getting what he wanted, and right now he wanted her to take this job. Worse, he might have sensed how much she wished she could do just that. And even worse than that the idea of Gabriel as a dinner companion held a temptation she didn't want to analyse.

'Well, that's no longer necessary, so I think we should change the seating plan back.'

'Why complicate matters?' A nod of his blond head showed that most of the guests had found their places. 'Come on—it won't be that bad. I promise I won't mention the job again. We can chat about whatever you like.'

Clearly he'd found the charm button again. The persuasive lilt to his deep voice and the accompanying smile held definite appeal, enticing her own lips into an answering upturn.

Careful, Etta. Perhaps he believed he could charm her into the job. Perhaps she should prove him wrong. Etta Mason was impervious to beguilement—had long since accepted that romance was not in her nature, that relationships were not something she understood. So…

'Fine.'

Once at their table, she turned to greet the man on her other side, received his congratulations on her speech, and realised from the slight slurring of his words that he was on the road to inebriation. No matter—she'd manage. Because no way did she want to give Gabriel Derwent even a *hint* of encouragement.

Within minutes she'd set Toby Davenport off on a conversational trail upon which he told her all about his expensive lifestyle, his luxury holidays, and his yacht. Which left Etta free to add the occasional comment of encouragement whilst she savoured the rich flavours of the venison broth, appreciated the authentic tang of cloves and mace from the medieval recipe, and did her best to ignore her body's hum of awareness at the warmth and sheer presence of Gabriel on her other side.

Until his well-modulated tones broke into the Davenport drone. 'Sounds amazing, Toby. Etta, here, is about to go on holiday. Tell me, Etta—I'm intrigued. As a historian, do you choose your holiday destinations based on historical interest? You mentioned a cruise… Where are you going?'

Etta opened her mouth and realisation dawned—she had no idea of the answer. Her mind was a resounding example of the clichéd blank state. When she'd booked the cruise its destination had been the least of her criteria—availability had been her priority, because the idea of a ship surrounded by sea had felt safe. That was why it had been worth the remortgaging of her flat and the ransacking of her savings to pay for it. Cathy would be safe from her father.

Because visceral fear had flared inside her—a fear that had been dormant for sixteen years but that had been reignited the instant Tommy had swaggered back into her life days before.

Focus, Etta. Gabe had raised his eyebrows, and his eyes were shadowed with concern.

'Sorry,' she managed. 'Senior moment. I can't remember.'

'You're too young to qualify.'

'Clearly not. I'll let you know if it comes back to me.'

Come on, Etta. Change the conversation. Unfortunately her brain was still tuned in to Planet Blank.

Desperation loosened her vocal cords as she saw the challenge in his eyes. 'In the meantime, what about *you*? Have you got any holiday plans for Christmas?'

'No. I'll be based at Derwent Manor. My parents are away in France, so my father can convalesce, and I need to ensure that various traditions are upheld. Including the annual Christmas Fair at the manor. This year I've decided to introduce a

Victorian theme—hopefully whoever I get to do the family tree can lend me some advice on that at the same time.'

Etta blinked. She *loved* to help with events such as this, and she'd bet Gabriel knew that. However innocent those blue-grey eyes looked as they calmly met her gaze.

'That sounds like a pretty full-on few weeks.' And a far cry from the playboy-style Christmas festivities she had imagined he would indulge in.

'It will be. In truth, running Derwent Manor is a full-time job in itself—my parents' whole life revolves around it.'

'And yours too?'

'Not my whole life, no.'

'But one day it will?'

'Yes.' The syllable was clipped, and she'd swear his knuckles had whitened around the crystal water tumbler he lifted to his lips.

'That must be strange. To always have known what your job will be one day. For most children the perennial question is, What do you want to be when you grow up? For royalty or aristocracy that isn't a question—you've always *known* what you will be when you grow up.'

'Yes.'

It was impossible to read anything from the single word—yet she sensed a depth of emotion in the sheer rigidity of his jaw. Did Gabriel Derwent relish or resent his destiny? Speaking of which…

'You said earlier that you believed in the power of choice over the power of fate, but that's not true, is it? Fate has decreed that you will become Duke of Fairfax.'

'Yes.' As if this time he'd realised the curtness of his response he curved his lips into the famous Derwent smile. 'But I do have the choice to renounce the title.'

Etta placed her spoon down into the empty bowl. 'Fair enough.' Even if she didn't believe he'd do that in a million years. 'But not everyone has that sort of choice. Think of all the princesses in history who were forced to marry. *They* had no choice.'

'You don't know that. You could argue that they simply chose to do their duty. And some of them could have elected to give their life up to religion. Sometimes none of the choices we have are palatable, but they exist.'

Etta opened her mouth but he raised a hand to forestall her.

'I know that there are examples of people who have no choice. Innocent people caught up in a chain of events they can't control. But I'm not sure fate comes into it—perhaps they are casualties of sheer bad luck.'

'Fate versus chance?' Even as she said the words Etta wondered how they had ended up in this discussion. It was almost as if they were in their own bubble amidst the glitz and buzz of their glamorous surroundings, complete with fairy-tale elements.

The warning bells that had clamoured earlier renewed their alarm. But there was no need for worry. Two more courses and she'd be on her way. She'd never meet Gabriel again. This conversation was nothing more than a welcome distraction from her thoughts of Tommy. That was all. A distraction. If Toby Davenport hadn't been bent on a drunken flirtation with his other neighbour she would no doubt have been distracted just as effectively by *him*.

Liar, liar, candy cane dress on fire.

In truth Gabriel Derwent was casting a mesh of fascination over both her body and her mind, and panic trickled through all the other sensations. She couldn't remember the last time her body had responded like this and she didn't like it.

Before Etta could end the conversation she felt her minuscule evening bag vibrate under the strategically placed napkin on her lap. Foreboding shivered her skin even as she tried to tell herself it could be anyone. There was no reason to believe anything had happened to Cathy.

Pushing her chair back, she tried to force her lips into a semblance of smile. 'Excuse me. I'll be back in a minute.'

Don't run.

CHAPTER THREE

GABE GLANCED AT the empty space next to him and frowned. No bathroom break took *this* long. Euphemistically speaking, Etta Mason could have powdered a hundred noses by now. Plus her food would soon congeal. Could she be in trouble?

Not his business. And yet there had been an expression of near fear on her face when she'd left the table, and that had touched him on a primitive level. Fear had once been a part of *his* life, and the memories still lingered in the recesses of his soul. Plus, the more he could discover about Etta Mason the more likely it would be that he could work out a way to persuade her to do the job. All valid reasons to go and check up on her.

Rising, he smiled at his table companions. 'Be back in a second.'

He moved through the imposing doors and into the hall. A quick scan showed no sign of Etta. Could be she had headed somewhere more private to make a call. Could be he should just leave her to it. Yet his feet strode towards the lobby, which was a fusion of medieval detail and modern comfort.

He halted on the threshold, took in the scene with lightning assessment. Etta was backed up against a pillar and a dark-haired man stood over her, aggression in his stance. The man's expression held a malevolent smirk that Gabe recognised as that of a bully, of a man who knew he inspired fear in his victim. Tattoos snaked and writhed over the bulge of muscles that spoke of a lot of time spent pumping iron.

'Is everything all right, Etta?' Stupid question, because Etta Mason looked like a different woman from the professional, articulate, give-as-good-as-you-get woman he'd sat with at dinner. Her face was pale, her hands were clenched, and those tawny brown eyes held a mix of defiance and fear.

'Everything's fine,' the man said. 'So you can take a hike.'

'I didn't ask *you*.'

The man took a step away from Etta. 'And...?' The menace was palpable. 'I said take a hike.'

Etta moved towards the man, her whole being diminished as she approached him, fear in every awkward movement, and Gabe knew with ice-cold certainty that at some point this man had hurt her.

'Tommy, please.'

The man gave a short, harsh laugh that prickled Gabe's skin.

'That sounds just like the old days, Etta.'

'Enough.' Cold rage ran through Gabe's veins and he strode towards Tommy. 'The only person who needs to take a hike round here is *you*.'

'It's OK, Gabe. I've got this.' Etta hauled in an audible breath. 'Tommy, just go. Please. You've made your point.'

Tommy hesitated, his dark eyes mean, his fists still clenched, and Gabe took another step forward.

Then, 'Fine. This toff isn't worth messing up my parole for. But this isn't over. Cathy is *my* daughter and I *will* meet her. Whatever it takes.' Turning, Tommy walked towards the portcullis-style door and exited.

Gabe turned to Etta. 'Are you all right?'

'Yes. Thank you.'

She rubbed her hands up and down her forearms and stared at the door as if to make sure Tommy had gone for good.

'Right.' Straightening, she tugged out her phone. 'I need to go.' A tap of her finger and then she lifted the phone to her ear. 'There's been a problem. Tommy turned up here. I'm on my way back now. I'll let you know what train I'm on.'

She glanced towards Gabe as if she was surprised he was still there and then she returned her attention to her phone.

'Taxi numbers...' she muttered under her breath.

'Where are you going?'

'London.'

Before he could even consider the import of his words his lips opened. 'I'll drive you there.'

Genuine shock made her jaw drop. 'Why would you do that?'

'Because I can get you to London way faster than the train, and I don't trust Tommy not to be waiting out there to follow you.'

The idea made her wince, and she rubbed her hands up and down her arms again, her brown eyes staring at a scenario that she clearly didn't like the look of. 'I'm not sure I should say yes, or why you even care, but I'd be a fool to refuse. Thank you.'

'Let's go. I'll find Ruby and explain you've had a family emergency.'

Ten minutes later Etta eyed Gabriel Derwent's deep red Ferrari and wondered anew if she shouldn't have caught a train, tried to hire a car—worked out some way to deal with this crisis herself. But the primitive need to be with Cathy overrode all else.

Logic told her that Cathy was safe with her friend Stephanie and her daughter Martha—according to Steph, Cathy and Martha were safely ensconced in Martha's bedroom, watching a rom-com. Common sense reinforced the idea—there was no way that Tommy could track Cathy down there. And yet he'd found Etta.

Chill, Etta. That was hardly a huge feat of deduction. Her website had detailed her speech at the Cavershams' Advent Ball. As for her mobile number—anyone could get that from her work answer-machine. But she couldn't 'chill'—not when she remembered how she had cringed before Tommy and his delight in her reaction. Dammit, he'd *revelled* in her fear—a fear that filled her with self-loathing even as a tidal wave of memories threatened to break lockdown. *No.* The past was over. She had to focus on the present and her daughter.

So Etta wanted to be with Cathy as soon as possible and Gabriel's car offered the ideal solution. The problem was Gabriel himself came with the deal.

'All set?' The deep timbre of his voice held concern alongside a hint of amusement. 'You're looking at the car as if it's akin to a lion's den.'

Heat warmed her cheeks. 'I'm just wondering whether it's fair to put you to so much trouble.'

'I offered.'

This was daft—and a waste of valuable time. A nod and then she pulled the low-slung door open and slid into the luxurious leather seat. Fact: Cathy was more important than anything else right now.

Within minutes they were on the road. Etta looked into the shadowy darkness as the powerful car ate up the miles. Wind turbines loomed in the dark, turned by the Cornish winds, fields and farmhouses flashed past, and occasionally she glanced at Gabriel Derwent. His blond hair gleamed in the moonlight, and his focus was on the road, each movement easy and competent.

He glanced at her too, then returned his attention to the deserted road. 'I get the feeling you're not comfortable. Are you worried about your daughter?'

'Yes. But I know she's safe. You'll have to let me pay you for this. I've dragged you away from an incredible dinner and moonlit dancing. I feel bad.'

'I told you. No need. Do you want to talk about it? The situation with Tommy and your daughter?'

Did she? For an odd moment a pull to do just that touched her. More madness—this man was a stranger, and not even her closest friends knew about that dark period of her life. 'There's nothing to say that you haven't deduced. You heard Tommy. He is Cathy's dad and he has decided he wants to see her. I don't want him anywhere near her.'

A small frown creased his forehead. Presumably he was wondering how she could ever have been such a fool as to have anything to do with a lowlife like Tommy.

'Has he ever been part of her life?'

'No.' Etta shook her head. 'I don't want to sound rude, but I don't want to talk about it.'

For years she had shut down the memories of Tommy and she had no wish to revisit them now—to expose her youthful stupidity, folly and weakness to this man. A man who clearly didn't know the definition of the word *weak*. Even now her insides felt coated with a fuzz of shame at her own behaviour, so best to keep the door firmly closed and padlocked with a host of security outside.

'This is my problem and I am dealing with it.'

'By running away on a cruise?'

Despite the softness of his deep voice, the words

sent a flare of anger through her. 'I am *not* running away.' *Was she?*

'I'm sorry if that sounded harsh, and I know I don't know the details. I get you don't want to discuss them. But if there is one lesson I've learnt in life it's that running away is seldom the best option.'

No doubt it was easy not to run away when you were the Earl of Wycliffe. Etta bit the words back—the man was doing her a massive favour here. 'Thanks for the advice. As I said, it's my problem and I'm dealing with it.'

With that Etta leant back and turned her head to focus on the landscape. Conversation over. To her relief Gabriel Derwent let it rest. Even if she sensed that next to her he was still mulling over the situation.

But he remained silent until they approached the outskirts of London, where he simply asked for directions, and soon enough they pulled up outside Steph's house.

'Thank you again. I truly appreciate this and I owe you a big favour.' The idea was an irritant that she suspected would stay with her until she worked out how to repay the debt. 'In the meantime, I wish you a safe journey home and I apologise again for wrecking your night.'

'I'll see you to the door.'

'No! Really… Steph is waiting up and I'd rather go in quietly.' She pushed open the door hurriedly. 'Goodbye, Gabriel.'

Without looking back she scurried up the stairs and pulled out the spare key Steph had given her. Right now she just wanted to go and see Cathy and watch her daughter breathe peacefully. Yet at the door she turned for one last glimpse at Gabriel Derwent's shadowy profile.

'How did you sleep?'

Etta looked up from the pine kitchen table and smiled at her best friend. 'Fine.'

'Fibber,' Steph said. 'You must have been terrified when Tommy appeared.'

'It was scary, but…' *But from the second Gabriel Derwent had appeared she had felt safe.*

She had to get a grip—life had taught her that the only person to rely on was herself. She'd escaped Tommy once—she'd do it again.

'I'll be fine.' Etta gripped her mug of coffee and tried hard to believe her words even as she heard the hollowness of each syllable. 'How was Cathy last night?'

'Quiet. She didn't mention Tommy to me,

though I'm sure she has talked to Martha about it. She *did* say she doesn't want to go on the cruise.'

Etta sighed. Her usually cheerful, well-behaved daughter had changed since Tommy's arrival on the scene, and Etta couldn't blame her—she herself would do anything to meet her own birth dad. Or mum.

She hadn't even known of their existence until she'd reached fifteen and discovered the fact that she'd been adopted. Worked out that her whole life had been an illusion, a lie. That was why she had vowed never to lie to Cathy, believed that honesty was the best way forward. So as Cathy had grown up Etta had told her who her dad was in an age-appropriate way. She had never wanted Cathy to feel she'd been lied to—hadn't wanted her daughter to build up a fantasy picture of her father. Equally, when Tommy had turned up with his demand to see his daughter, Etta had told Cathy the truth—but she hadn't anticipated her daughter's reaction.

Cathy, caught in a web of confused emotions, wanted her father to be a wonderful man. Wanted to meet him, to bond with him, and the idea sent waves of terror through Etta's veins. No one knew better than she the spell Tommy could exert when he wanted to—she could imagine his spin, the story of his reformation, his interpretation of his past character as misunderstood rebel without a cause.

She gusted out a sigh as she looked at Steph. 'I know she doesn't want to go.' But the cruise had to happen, because Etta would not—could not— sit back and watch her daughter repeat her own mistakes. 'But we're going anyway.' She rose to her feet. 'Thanks a million for last night, hun. There's no need for you to stay. I know you need to get Martha to her singing lesson.'

'Stay here as long as you like.'

Twenty minutes later the click of the front door indicated their departure and Etta approached the bedroom where Cathy was staying.

Her daughter sat cross-legged on the bed, her long dark hair pulled back in a ponytail set high on her head. 'Mum—please, please, *please* don't make me go on this cruise. If Dad wants to see me badly enough to follow you to Cornwall then surely it's worth a try.'

Etta sensed her daughter's frustration and it tore her apart. 'Sweetheart, your father is not a safe person to be around.'

'Maybe he's changed.'

Before Etta could answer, the doorbell pealed

and fear jumped up her throat. *Keep calm.* No way could it be Tommy.

Cathy leapt off the bed, clearly desperate for the very thing that held Etta petrified to the spot.

'Cathy—wait!'

Ungluing her feet from the carpet, Etta raced down the stairs after her daughter, reaching the bottom just as Cathy got to the door and peered through the spyhole.

'It's not Dad. It's some blond bloke.'

Disappointment drooped Cathy's shoulders and Etta moved forward and pulled her into a quick hug, her heart aching even as relief surged through her.

Cathy stepped back. 'We'd better open the door. Whoever it is he looks familiar. Good-looking for his age.'

Etta peeped through the spyhole and blinked. Blinked again in case of hallucination. But Gabriel Derwent remained in her line of vision. Casually dressed in jeans and a long-sleeved sweatshirt, he still exuded an energy that sent her pulse-rate up a notch. Be that as it may, she couldn't leave him standing on Steph's doorstep.

She pulled the door open and bit back a protest as he stepped forward and closed the door behind him.

'What…?'

'Apologies for the unannounced visit. There's been a development.'

'I don't understand,' Etta said, as foreboding prickled her skin. Surely things couldn't get any worse. *Could* they? 'What sort of a development?'

CHAPTER FOUR

GABRIEL HALTED, ALL thoughts of developments scrambled in his brain as he gazed at Etta. This was a completely different Etta from the previous night, and somehow even more full of allure in jeans and a short knitted cream jumper that emphasised the length of her legs. Shower-damp chestnut hair emitted a tantalising waft of strawberry, and fell in a glossy swathe around her unmade-up face. Her skin glowed and a smattering of freckles down the bridge of her nose was now revealed. For an absurd second his hands tingled with the urge to reach out and run his finger down the line. As for her lips—

Hurriedly he tore his gaze away and realised that they weren't alone.

A girl stepped closer to Etta and eyed him with a speculative gaze. There could be no doubt the two were related, despite the girl's long curtain of dark hair; her eyes were the same amber-flecked brown. Sisters? Or…

Etta stepped forward. 'Gabriel, this is my daughter, Cathy. Cathy, this is Gabriel—the man who kindly drove me home last night.'

Her chin tilted upwards as she met his gaze in an unspoken challenge, and he blinked away the surprise he knew had surfaced in his eyes. There was no point in pretence—he *was* surprised. In his mind Cathy had been considerably younger, and his brain whirred to adjust the parameters of the idea he intended to present to Etta.

'Good to meet you,' he said, and he held out a hand to Cathy, who surveyed him, her dark head tilted to one side.

'Are you...Gabriel Derwent?'

'The one and only.'

They were words he wished unsaid as he flinched inwardly at their bleak truth. One day he *could* be the one and only Duke of Fairfax— the last of the line. Yet he forced his lips to tilt upwards and could only hope the smile factor outweighed the grimace.

A small frown etched Etta's forehead. 'Cathy, could you go and get ready, please? Once Gabriel has left we need to get home and pick up our cases.'

Cathy heaved a sigh. 'I *told* you, Mum. It's not *necessary*. We don't need to *go*.' The muttered words held defiance underlain with resignation, but she headed for the staircase.

'Cathy. We'll discuss this later, but the bottom line is we *are* going.'

Once the teenager had trailed up the stairs Etta turned to Gabe. Her lips parted as if to speak but instead she just stared at him for a moment, her eyes wide.

Then she stepped back and gave her head a small shake. 'Look, I don't want to be rude, but I haven't got a lot of time. The cruise leaves to-night. What's happened?'

This would be a tricky conversation, and he'd be damned if he would conduct it in a hallway. 'I appreciate that you're busy, but we do need to talk. Properly. With you focused on what I have to say. I promise I will be succinct.'

A hesitation, and then she nodded. 'OK. Come through to the kitchen. I'll make coffee. It sounds like I'll need it.'

Gabe followed Etta into a spacious, airy kitchen with cheerful daffodil-yellow walls adorned with corkboards holding pinned artwork and photos. He seated himself at a big wooden table as she filled the old-fashioned kettle.

'OK. Hit me with it.'

Easy does it, Gabe. Instinct told him Etta

wouldn't appreciate his next words, however he spun them.

'The press clocked our departure from the ball last night, found out about our moonlit stroll on the terrace and discovered my ploy with the seating plan. They have decided you and I are an item. I thought I'd better give you the heads-up as there may be reporters outside your house.'

For a second she stood as if frozen, her lips formed in a circle of astonishment, her head tilted, waiting for the punchline. Then, when she realised none was forthcoming, she banged the kettle down onto the hob and sheer outrage etched her cheekbones with a flush of anger.

'*You* and *me*? The press thinks *we* are an item?'

Hmm... A hint of chagrin touched him at the sheer horror that laced her voice. 'I'm afraid so.'

Jeez, was it that bad?

'But that's ludicrous!'

'Why?' It wasn't what he had meant to say, but her expression of distaste had sparked a surge of irritation.

'Because…because it is such an impossible scenario.'

'Why?' Rising to his feet, he headed towards the kitchen counter, kept his gaze on hers.

And suddenly the atmosphere hitched up a

notch. Or three. The look of aversion faded from her face and morphed into shock as desire ignited in her eyes. Gabe's mouth dried, and the tick-tock of a clock in the background pounded his eardrums as he moved closer—close enough that those damned freckles caught his attention again.

Her hands gripped the underside of the worktop so tightly her knuckles showed white against the marbled grey. As if the touch had pulled her back to reality she stepped back. 'It's impossible because it could never happen.' The quaver in her voice demonstrated the shakiness of her argument.

'Really?' He pulled his phone out and tapped the screen. 'Look.'

Etta stared at the images, and Gabe could almost see her eyeballs pop from their sockets on cartoon stalks as she swore under her breath.

'Yup. That's what *I* thought.' Gabe couldn't keep the smugness from his voice. Because some enterprising photographer had captured the moment he and Etta had met, as she'd emerged from behind the potted plant. There could be no denying the look of utter arrest on their faces.

'I'll track down whoever took that and disembowel him,' Etta muttered, before looking up with a tilt of her chin and challenge in her eyes. 'Because he is incompetent—clearly the light was odd, or the angle of the lens, or...or...'

'Or we saw each other and there was a mutual moment of appreciation.'

Her eyes rested on his image and for a heartbeat he would have sworn there was a glimpse of satisfaction on her face at seeing him equally smitten. Then it was gone and she straightened up.

'I'll stick to the mistake theory, thank you.'

Gabe raised his eyebrows. Maybe he should have let it go, but her sheer refusal to acknowledge the attraction prompted curiosity—along with his inner devil. 'Or you could admit the truth. You are attracted to me and vice versa. I don't have an issue acknowledging it.' He gestured to the screen. 'The evidence is right there.'

If the laws of physics had allowed, her laser glare would have shot his phone with its telltale images to smithereens. 'This may be hard for you to believe, but *I am not attracted to you.*'

Each word was exaggerated, and issued through clenched teeth, and yet Gabe knew she was lying.

'You don't *want* to be attracted to me.' And he wasn't sure why not. 'That's different.'

'Gabriel...'

'Please. Only my parents call me Gabriel. I prefer Gabe.'

'Gabe. You are not my type. I don't go for shallow playboys or men who lead women on and then break their hearts.'

Whoa. '"Shallow playboy" I'll own up to. But I don't lead women on.' *Ever.*

'What about Lady Isobel? You led that poor woman up the garden path, round the garden and a whole village full of houses. You made her think you'd marry her, then you bailed out in the public eye, broke her heart and humiliated her.'

Anger stirred inside him even as he accepted Etta's stance—Isobel had played her part to perfection, and most of the country believed in her false portrayal of Gabe Derwent as heartbreaker extraordinaire. In return she'd netted herself a packet and some great publicity. A month after that his sister Kaitlin had spotted her partying on the Riviera. It seemed as if Isobel had decided to break free—rebel against the role of duchess she'd been primed for and go for the money.

But forget Isobel. Right now Etta glared at him, one foot tapping the kitchen floor tiles. Gabriel met her gaze full on. 'I thought historians valued accuracy and confirmation and didn't rely on tabloid gossip?'

Heat touched her cheeks. 'A good historian looks at the available evidence and makes deductions. Are you denying that you led Lady Isobel to think you would marry her?'

'No. I'm not. But that is one fact. There are a whole host of other facts you are not privy to. Unlike Isobel, I intend to keep them private. However, I give you my word that it did not go down the way she claimed it did. I didn't break her heart.'

A pause, and then she lifted her shoulders in a small shrug. 'I accept that I may not know the full story. But I'm *still* not attracted to you. I appreciate you coming to warn me, and I'll explain to any reporters it's all a misunderstanding.'

'Actually, I have a different solution.'

Suspicion narrowed her eyes. 'We don't need a different solution. We don't need any solution because this doesn't need to be a problem.'

'Fine. I have an *idea* I want to run by you. It benefits us both.'

The kettle whistled as she hesitated, and then she pulled a cafetière towards her and nodded. 'OK. Shoot. You've got a cup of coffee's worth of time.'

'Seems fair. I suggest we go along with the press. Run with the story.'

Her hand jolted on the plunger at his words and coffee spilt onto the counter. Etta ignored it. *'Go along with it? Run with the story?'* Her hands tipped in an exaggerated question. *'Why?* Why would we even do a two-minute walk with the story?'

'Because as my girlfriend you can bring Cathy and move in to Derwent Manor with me. You can put together the family tree. In return I will pay you a hefty fee and keep you safe from Tommy. Win-win.'

This way he would get his family tree done by the expert he wanted, she would get the chance to complete a project he knew she wanted, and she would be safe from Tommy. He figured it was pure genius. Etta looked at him as if she thought it was sheer garbage.

'That's nuts.'

'No, it isn't.'

'Yes, it is. For a start, how can you possibly guarantee our safety?'

'I have a number of qualifications in self-defence and a variety of martial arts.'

Once Gabe had worked out that no one was going to rescue him from the horrors of boarding school and the ritual humiliation the other students felt a prospective duke deserved, he'd figured he needed to rescue himself. The best way to do that had been to learn self-defence—and as it turned out he had an aptitude for it.

Etta shook her head, clearly unimpressed by the claim as she mopped up the spilt coffee and poured the remains into two mugs. 'You don't get it. Tommy is a nutcase. He's a street fighter. He got put away for an assortment of crimes—drug-dealing, armed robbery, and a hit-and-run whilst fleeing the scene of a crime.'

'I'm not belittling any of that, and I'm not blowing hot air—I *can* protect you from Tommy. I didn't just do a few classes and get a few belts. I'm the real McCoy. There is no way I would offer protection if I wasn't one hundred per cent sure I could provide it.'

Her fingers drummed a tattoo on the counter, and her head tilted to one side as her brown eyes assessed him. 'It wouldn't work.'

'Why not?'

'You couldn't protect both Cathy *and* me because we won't be together all the time. Plus…' Her voice trailed off.

Gabe stared at her as his mind trawled the brief time he'd spent with Cathy. 'Plus Cathy doesn't want to go on the cruise because she wants to meet her Dad, and that would make her difficult to protect?' he surmised.

For a moment he thought she wouldn't answer, and then she exhaled on a sigh. 'Yes. Which is why the cruise is a good idea.'

'You can't keep Cathy on a ship in the middle of an ocean for ever.'

'I know that. But right now it works for me as a strategy.'

'I told you yesterday—running away is seldom a good strategy.' He had a memory of his eight-year-old self—the sheer exhilaration that had streamed through his body as he'd escaped boarding school. The terrified but determined trek home to Derwent Manor, the blisters on his aching feet, the growl of hunger in his stomach. His ignominious reception.

'Derwents do not run, Gabriel. You have let the Derwent name down.'

His explanation about the bullying had fallen on deaf ears.

'Cowardice cannot be tolerated, Gabriel.'

'This is a tactical retreat.'

'Don't kid yourself, Etta. A tactical retreat is a chance to move away so that you can regroup, because to stand your ground means certain defeat. You can't regroup on a cruise ship.'

Her mug made a decisive *thunk* on the counter. 'Enough. I've known you for less than twenty-four hours—I don't need your advice or analysis. This doesn't even make sense. There are other historians you could employ in a way that's much more straightforward and considerably less dangerous. *Why* offer to do this at all?'

It was a good question. From the second he'd seen her with Tommy a protective urge had kicked in. Nothing personal, but born from his own childhood experience of bullying, the taste of helplessness, the shameful desire to flee.

'My instinct tells me you are the right person for the job, and I don't like men like Tommy so it would be a great pleasure to kick him round the block. Several times.'

Her expression warmed even as she shook her head. 'That is a wonderful thought, but it won't work. I need Cathy off Tommy's radar.'

'Fair enough.' Turning, he paced the length of the counter. 'How about you stay here and Cathy goes on the cruise? With grandparents or another family member? I'll pay any difference.'

'There *are* no other family members.' Etta's voice was flat, clipped with sadness. 'Which is fine, because *I* will keep Cathy safe.'

'The best way to do that is to deal with Tommy.'

A small sigh escaped her lips and for a heart-beat vulnerability gleamed in the brown depths of her eyes, as if the idea of dealing with Tommy scared her.

'Whilst *I* keep you safe.'

Once again her fingers drummed on the counter-top. 'I could ask Steph if she would take Cathy. And Martha, of course. The girls are at college together. I've explained the situation to the head and he is all right with me taking Cathy out as long as she takes some work with her. Martha could do the same. Steph is a self-employed il-lustrator, so she may be able to take work with her...' Etta shook her head. 'Sorry. I'm thinking out loud here.'

'That's fine with me.'

'I'll talk to Cathy first, and then Steph. *If* they agree I'll research your family tree and in return you will pay me and act as my bodyguard whilst I figure out how to deal with Tommy.'

'And we'll go along with the press angle of a romance between us.'

When he'd seen the article that morning his first thought had been that he'd better warn Etta. His next had been to consider whether this develop-ment might be utilised to his advantage. His *and* Etta's. After all, an alliance only worked if it ben-efited both parties.

'It works for us both.'

'How do you figure that?' Her voice held a certain fascinated curiosity.

'If the press believes we're dating it takes the spotlight away from you researching the new family tree. No one need even know that I am hiring you.' *Nor start to dig into my motivation for doing so.*

Besides, if his father got wind of his supposed 'surprise gift' he'd know something was off—neither the Duke nor Duchess had any interest in the family tree except in that it showed the unbroken direct line that he was about to snap with heart-rending finality.

'That hardly works for *me*. If I am working for you then I want recognition for that.'

'And you can have that recognition. In spades and shovels and pitchforks. After Christmas.'

'A fat lot of good it will do me then. By then my professional reputation will be in ruins. It will look as though you hired me because I was sleeping with you.'

A pause stretched into a silence and for a second Gabe knew with bone-deep certainty that their minds had tracked the same path to an image of silken sheets and bare skin, of touch and taste and…

'Supposedly,' Etta said, her voice a touch breathy. '*Supposedly* sleeping with you.'

'Not when they see your credentials and the results you provide. No one will blame you for mixing business and pleasure—you can spin the whole girlfriend deal into positive publicity. This is an opportunity.' One that any woman he had ever dated had *always* taken advantage of—a chance to glean celebrity coverage and rich pickings.

Her mouth opened in a circle of outrage. 'So you see this as a deal-sweetener?'

Gabe shrugged. 'Yes.'

'Not for me. I'd rather earn positive publicity through my *work*. So thanks, but no, thanks. I'll do your family tree. But I won't be your girlfriend. Fake or otherwise.' Her chin tilted in challenge. 'Take it or leave it.'

There was no quarter in her words and a hint of chagrin touched his nerves…along with a small burn of surprise. Not that it mattered. The most important objective had been achieved and he was a step closer to finding a future Derwent heir.

'I'll take it. We can tell the press I'm hiring you as a consultant for the Christmas Fair.' Yet her continued refusal to acknowledge their attraction prompted his vocal chords. 'But any time you change your mind and want to be my girlfriend—fake or otherwise—let me know. We can play this any way you want. It's up to you.'

CHAPTER FIVE

'*ANY TIME YOU change your mind and want to be my girlfriend—fake or otherwise—let me know.*'

The words, uttered in tones of molten chocolate, buzzed around Etta's brain and demolished each and every brain cell in their path.

Their whole conversation, with its undertone of awareness, had sent her body into overdrive. Her whole being tingled, sparkled, as sensations tap-danced on her skin.

Get a grip. Of some form of sanity.

Flirting with Gabriel Derwent was idiocy—the man had a master's degree in the art and she didn't hold so much as a pass. Yet her imagination danced with the possible scenario—what would he do if she took him up on the 'otherwise' option? Chose to join the ranks of his playboy play dates…? *Yuck*, said the tiny part of her brain that advocated logic and common sense. *Yum*, shrieked her hormones, dizzy at the prospect.

The atmosphere in the room had accelerated to

steamy and Gabe was so close. His eyes were dark with desire…dark as the blue of a storm-tossed sea. Breathing seemed problematic, time slowed in direct correlation to the leap in her pulse and her lips parted in anticipation.

Then guilt slammed in. *What am I doing?* Attraction led to loss of perspective, made you behave in ways so stupid and alien they changed your life, caused pain and loss. Already for long moments she had taken her eye off the most important issue: Cathy.

Pressing her lips together, she moved away from him, all too aware of the telltale jerkiness of her movements. *Focus, Etta.* No way would she give Gabriel Derwent any power over her—she would not relinquish even a jot of control. To any man. *Ever.* She'd experienced powerlessness first-hand already. Never again.

'I don't want to play at all. I want to keep my daughter safe. I'll let you know what is happening once I've spoken to Cathy and Steph. Provided all goes to plan, I'll travel down to Derwent Manor once Cathy is safely gone.' Holding out a hand she waited expectantly, but Gabriel didn't move to take it.

'I'm not going anywhere. Whatever happens, you need to go home to get your suitcases. There's a chance Tommy will be there, and it's a definite that the press will be. So I'll go with you. I'm your bodyguard, Etta, so you'd better get used to me.'

Just fabulous.

'And speaking of the press conference,' he continued smoothly. 'We'd better discuss a strategy. That photograph needs to be explained.'

There seemed little point in a reiteration of her the-photographer-got-it-wrong defence because it sucked. The previous night she'd thought she'd been poleaxed when she first saw him. Well, that was a freaking understatement—if she looked closely at that picture she'd probably spot the drool on her chin. Though at least Gabe looked similarly afflicted, and despite herself there was that funny little thrill. *Again.*

'I…' In truth she couldn't think of a single explanation, and he knew it. A smile quirked his lips and she was tempted to kick him in the shin. *Hard.* 'We need to stress that our association is strictly professional. That you are hiring me as a consultant for the Christmas Fair.'

'And hope they believe us and don't pick up on our body language?'

'There *is* no body language.'

'You're one hundred per cent sure of that?'

'One hundred and ten,' she stated. 'So there will be nothing for the press to pick up on.'

Even if she had to douse herself in an ice bath before meeting them.

'I'll go and talk to Cathy and then call Steph.'

Gabe watched Etta leave and felt intrigue mingle with surprise—most women would have taken him up on his offer. Especially given the flare of mutual attraction. For a second disappointment lingered at her refusal to acknowledge it, let alone act on it. But there would be other women—right now his focus was on business, not pleasure, so really he should feel relief at her decision to keep their relationship professional.

Glancing round Steph's kitchen, Gabe saw that Etta featured in the collage of photographs—an absurdly young-looking Etta with a woman he presumed to be Steph posing at a carousel. Etta held a dark-haired toddler, a miniature version of today's Cathy, and Steph held a blonde little girl of a similar age. There was another picture of the two women with their girls in school uniform, beaming with similar gap-toothed grins at the camera.

Gabe felt a two pronged searing of loss—for a past he couldn't change and a future he wouldn't have. The only photos he had of himself with his mother were publicity shots, and he would have no children to be pictured with. Fate had decreed that his body would let him down and the Derwent line would end. But perhaps there was still hope—perhaps there was another heir out there and Etta would find him. *That* was the goal.

As if on cue, the kitchen door opened to reveal Etta.

'Steph and Martha are thrilled, and Cathy is at least more enthusiastic than she was. Though she wants to speak to you alone. I don't know why. Maybe she wants to make sure you won't beat Tommy up too badly. Or—' she gave a sudden smile '—maybe she's checking you out as a suitable person for me to stay with.'

'I'll assure her that my intentions are strictly honourable.' *More's the pity*, whispered his libido.

Five minutes later Cathy entered the room and headed to the large wooden table in the window alcove. Gabe seated himself opposite her and waited as she surveyed him. Her assessment was direct, as if she were trying to decide how to play him. Fair play to her—it would be his own strategy in her place.

'So Mum will be staying with you?'

'Yes.'

'And you will protect her from my dad?'

'Yes.'

'It won't be necessary.' Cathy's chin tilted at an angle that mirrored Etta's line of stubbornness. 'Dad just wants to see *me*. I don't get what's so bad about that. He has changed over the past sixteen years. You'd think Mum would be glad.'

'I saw your dad last night, Cathy, and he struck me as potentially dangerous.'

For a nanosecond doubt entered her eyes, and then she shook her head. 'We're all *potentially* dangerous. Dad wouldn't hurt me. Or Mum.'

'Your mum is just looking out for you.'

'I get that. But I'm *sixteen*. Mum was pregnant with me when she was my age, and she had no one. She's always said she got where she is because people took a chance on her. So why won't she give Dad a chance?'

Gabe sensed deep waters closing in over his head. 'Cathy, this is something you should discuss with your mum, not me.'

'But I won't be *able* to discuss it with her because *I'll* be in the middle of the ocean. *You'll* be with Mum whilst *she* is dealing with Dad. You could help me, seeing as I've helped you.'

This was a girl after his own heart—a girl who

saw the value of quid pro quo. 'How do you work that out?'

'You really want Mum for this job, and I could have got her to turn it down.'

'You could have,' he agreed. 'But it's not my place to influence your mum's decisions. I'm her employer. Plus, I'm sure your mum knows what she's doing with regard to your father.'

Cathy shook her head. 'Once Mum makes up her mind she digs her heels in. She'll never admit she's wrong about Dad. *Never.* Especially not if everyone keeps agreeing with her. *You* managed to persuade her to take your job instead of coming on this cruise. That's, like, *incredible.* You could try and persuade her to give Dad a chance.'

'I'm sorry, Cathy, but no can do. This is between your mum and you.'

A knock on the door interrupted them and Gabe turned his head to see Etta approaching the table. She looked professional from the tips of her smooth short chestnut hair that curved to touch the hollows of her shoulder blades to the tips of her black buttoned boots. The tailored two-toned blue tweed jacket worn over a matching dress gave a stylish twist to her authority. Seamed at the waist, the sophisticated shift with its V neckline emphasised both her slenderness and her curves and Gabe's breath caught in his throat.

'Sorry to interrupt, but Steph and Martha are back and we need to go and get our suitcases. And face the press.'

Cathy rose from her chair and threw one last glance of appeal at Gabe. 'At least promise you'll think about what I've said.'

'Think about what?' Etta asked, once her daughter had left the room, and then she shook her head. 'Forget I asked. That's not fair. Cathy wanted to speak with you privately. Just promise me she hasn't got any hare-brained schemes in her head.'

'If she has she didn't confide them to me. Plus, short of swimming the ocean, I can't see there is much she can do.'

'That's true.' Smoothing her skirt down, she hauled in a breath. 'So, shall we go?'

'Yes.' He rose to his feet and saw the pallor of her face. 'You don't need to be nervous.'

'Actually, I think I do. A certifiable nutter may well be lurking amongst that throng of press sniffing out a non-existent story.'

'The press will work in our favour. The last thing Tommy will want, if he is serious about seeing Cathy, is any confrontation recorded by the

press. Plus, late last night he was in Cornwall—
my guess is he won't have made it back here yet.'

'That's true.'

Etta looked marginally more cheerful, and a
funny feeling of satisfaction that he'd erased at
least one line from her furrowed brow touched
his chest.

'Odds are he's sleeping off a session in the pub
as well. He'd already been drinking when he
found me.'

A small shudder shivered through her, as if the
words had triggered a memory she'd rather forget.
Gabe's guess was that Tommy was a mean drunk
and his fists clenched—with any luck Tommy
would turn up, and Gabe could make him wish
he hadn't.

In the meantime… 'Don't mention Cathy to the
press at all. The implication for Tommy will be
that Cathy is with you at Derwent Manor—that
way he won't try anything when she's en route to
the cruise. And keep an eye out for April Fotherington—she's a good reporter but she'll be pushing the romance angle.'

'You can't push something that doesn't exist.'

Her tone brooked no argument.

One more sweep of her hand over her skirt and

she nodded. 'Let's do this. Sooner we go, the sooner it's over, right?'

'Right. Let's get this show on the road.'

'And it *was* a pretty impressive show,' Etta admitted later to Steph, even as reluctance twisted her tongue.

The press had adored him, had seemingly accepted their professional status, and had taken Gabe's assurance that, with his father so unwell, romance was the last thing on his mind. That all he wanted was to ensure the Derwent Manor Christmas Fair was an unparalleled success, so that the Duke of Fairfax could be reassured that all was well. And so he had hired Etta Mason, renowned historian, to help ensure that his Victorian theme was historically accurate.

Only April Fotherington had been a little sceptical, but she had backed down when Gabe had offered her exclusive coverage of the fair.

'In fact he turned the whole thing into a massive publicity stunt for the Christmas Fair.'

'Definitely impressive,' Steph said, with an approving nod of her ash-blond head. 'And that's because he's a pretty impressive guy.'

Her friend grinned in a way that Etta could only categorise as sly.

'I still don't fully understand why you didn't take him up on the girlfriend idea.'

There were still some idiotic seconds when Etta wondered the same thing. 'Because it would be wrong. On so many levels.'

'And right on *so* many others. Honest, hun, I think you are *mad*! Imagine what fun you could have had. The pictures in the magazines, the fancy dinners, romantic champagne-filled weekends away...'

Steph wiggled her eyebrows and despite herself Etta grinned even as she shook her head.

'I don't *do* romance, Steph. You know that.' Maybe Tommy had beaten it out of her. Maybe it was a missing gene. Inherited from the birth parents she'd never known.

'Forget romance—you could have had some *fun* as his fake girlfriend. You could have even more fun as his *real* girlfriend. I can tell you fancy him. Why not go for it?'

'I agree.'

Etta looked up as Cathy and Martha entered the room, laden with suitcases, and dropped them next to Steph and Martha's bright pink ones by the door.

'Steph's right,' Cathy continued. 'You *should* have some fun.' Cathy's pretty face grew serious as she came forward and perched on the arm of Etta's chair. 'Mum, I know how much you've done for me, and I know you missed out on loads of the fun that other teenagers and young women had because you were looking after me. Now's your chance to make up for it for a while. Have fun. Go to parties. Dress up. Dance the night away.'

'Cathy, sweetheart…' Her heart turned over with love for her daughter as she reached up to cup her face. 'I promise you that I have never once regretted all those nights of "fun" I supposedly missed out on. You are the very best thing that ever happened to me.'

That was the complete truth. Without Cathy, who knew whether she would have found the courage to leave Tommy, to run away in the depths of the night and find refuge on the streets. Without Cathy to care for would she have studied and worked and become the person she was? Probably not, was the answer.

'I don't need to dance the night away with anyone. Let alone Gabriel Derwent.'

As if on cue the doorbell rang, and Steph rose to answer it. Minutes later she ushered in Gabriel, followed by the tall, brown-haired Ethan Caversham.

Resolutely Etta kept her gaze on Ethan as she

rose to her feet, yet despite herself she felt her skin shiver in response to Gabe's proximity, her whole body on super-alert.

'Ethan, this is so kind of you.' Gabe had asked Ethan to drive Steph, Martha and Cathy to the cruise ship as an added precaution against Tommy. 'I can't thank you enough.'

'It's no problem. Ruby sends her love and says you have to come round for lunch soon.' His face softened when he mentioned his wife in exactly the same way Ruby's did when she mentioned Ethan, and it filled Etta with a strange yearning—the equivalent of a child with her nose pressed against a sweet shop window, knowing she couldn't have a single sugar-coated mouthful.

'Sounds great.'

But now it was time to say goodbye, and Etta felt tears prickle at the backs of her eyes as she turned to her daughter. She thanked her lucky stars that whatever genes she was missing she had never once had any inclination to abandon *this* precious part of her life.

'Cathy, sweetheart. Have fun, and take care, and listen to Steph, and do all your college work, and...'

Cathy hurtled into her arms and wrapped her arms around her waist. 'Mum, I'll be fine. *You* take care—and *you* look after her,' she added, turning to glare at Gabe.

'I will,' Gabe said, his voice serious, and Cathy gave a small satisfied nod.

Then, minutes later, they were gone.

Pull it together, Etta. This was the right thing to do. Her daughter would be safe. That was all that mattered.

'It's OK to be upset.'

Gabriel's voice held a sympathy that surprised and distracted her from thoughts of Cathy as she turned to face him.

'I know. And I know Cathy is sixteen—she's definitely old enough to do this. It's just that we've never been apart this long before. A weekend here and there, but otherwise it's been her and me all the way.'

His face held an unreadable expression, and a hint of sadness whispered through his eyes. 'Then she is very lucky.'

'I don't know... I've always felt bad that she doesn't have a family.' Familiar sorrow touched her that she'd been unable to provide Cathy with grandparents. Only birth parents who had abandoned Etta at a day old and adoptive parents who had turned her away when she'd refused to give up Cathy.

Your choice, Etta. We'll take you back, but surely you can't want to keep a child who carries that man's genes? Her adoptive mother's words had slammed her with clarity—the reason her parents hadn't been able to love her was because for all those years they'd raised her they had believed her to be tainted by the genes of her unknown birth parents.

Etta pushed the memories down fiercely—what was done was done. Over the years she had come to realise that her parents hadn't *chosen* not to love her. They had entered into adoption with every intention of loving her—had truly believed they could take in a child who didn't share their blood or genes. And maybe they *could* have loved a different child. Just not Etta.

Enough.

Such thoughts were unproductive at best, depressing at worst. Now she had Cathy, and that was all the family she needed. She had Steph, other friends, a career—a life that she had built brick by painstaking brick.

Etta lifted her shoulders. 'But it is as it is, and I know I'm lucky to have her. Cathy is a fabulous girl—really together, caring, bright—' She broke off. 'Sorry, I sound like one of those dreadful mothers who goes on and on about their precious little darlings.'

'No, you sound like someone who gets on well with her child, and that's something to be proud of.'

'Thank you. Cathy and I *do* get on well. That's why I'll miss her. Especially now, with the run-up to Christmas. We go a little Christmas mad—we decorate the flat to within an inch of its life and I get the biggest tree we can cram in. Oh, and last year we had an inflatable Rudolph on the patio. Hard to imagine, but there it is!'

Embarrassment struck. This man was an aristocrat. His Christmases were undoubtedly posh, expensive affairs, and here she was rabbiting on about plastic tat.

'Anyway, I'm sure your Christmas is far more sophisticated.'

A shrug greeted the comment. 'I'm not much of a Christmas person.'

Etta blinked. 'How can you *not* love Christmas?'

'It's not my thing.' His expression was closed, as if he regretted his admission. 'It's not a big deal.'

But it *was* a big deal. Christmas was about love and family and peace and goodwill. 'So how are you going to plan a Christmas fair if you're full of *Bah humbug* rather than Christmas cheer.'

'That's different. This fair has been an annual tradition at Derwent for the past one hundred and fifty years—since Victorian times. Which is why I am introducing a Victorian theme this year. It's never been themed before, but I think it will attract bigger crowds, which will mean more money coming in. There will be re-enactors, Victorian games for the children...'

His deep voice vibrated with enthusiasm, but more than that it resonated with determination that the fair would be a success—an extravaganza. Almost as if he wanted, *needed* to make a statement, to impose his own brand on the fair. Purpose showed on every hard plane of his face, and his attitude a far cry from that of an idle aristocrat. His sheer aura sent a frisson of an elusive something through her body.

'It sounds incredible, and I'll help in any way I can—especially as we've told the press that you're hiring me as a consultant. Plus, I'll need to get my Christmas fix from somewhere.'

'But your priority is the family tree.'

'Of course. The sooner I get started the happier I'll be.' In fact Etta realised she hadn't given any thought to what happened next, because somehow since Gabe's arrival into her life everything had moved so fast. Under *his* orders. 'So the sooner we set off to Derwent Manor the better.'

'We'll go tomorrow. It's better to stay in London tonight, until Ethan lets us know they are safely aboard. Just in case something unforeseen happens.'

Panic clutched her, tightened round her chest. 'You don't think Tommy could…?'

'Could have found out about the cruise? I don't see how, but it's best to be prepared for any contingency. If he *is* around, Ethan will deal with him.'

Curiosity flickered. 'So you and Ethan must be good friends?'

Was it her imagination or did he hesitate ever so imperceptibly before he answered.

'I only met him a couple of weeks ago. Cora knows the Cavershams well, so I asked her for an introduction in the hope of persuading them to give me an invitation to their Advent Ball. It snowballed from there.'

Curiosity bubbled. 'And on the back of that you asked him to drive Steph, Cathy and Martha to the cruise ship?'

'Yes.'

Etta waited, but clearly that was it.

Instead of elaborating Gabe glanced at his watch. 'If you're ready we should leave now. The hotel is booked.'

'I'll pay for it. We're only staying in London because of Cathy.'

'It's all part of the job package. The deal we have is all-expenses-paid, and we'll be discussing the parameters of the job over dinner.'

'But that doesn't seem fair—really, I'd rather pay...'

His eyebrows rose in a look of surprise that was almost comical—presumably he wasn't used to women offering to pay their own way. Yet if she didn't she would feel like one of *those* women, and the idea swirled in a conflict of sensation inside her tummy. His words still echoed her brain— *'Any time you change your mind and want to be my girlfriend—fake or otherwise—let me know.'*

Not happening.

'Really. Really. *Really.*'

Now amusement touched his face, and she knew he had read her mind. 'And *I'd* really, really, *really* prefer to pay myself. Don't worry—there is no hidden meaning to this. If it makes you feel better it's tax-deductible.'

Etta hesitated, then nodded. Perhaps she could

have a word with Reception and work out a way
to settle the bill once they got there.

As Gabe pulled into a space in a public car park
in central Mayfair he glanced across at Etta. 'It's
a minute's walk from here.'

'Where are we staying?

Snapping his seatbelt undone, Gabe named one
of London's most prestigious hotels.

'We can't stay *there*.'

'Why not?' No woman he knew would pass up
the opportunity.

'Because it will cost a fortune.'

'That is not your concern.' Though the muti-
nous line of her lips indicated otherwise. 'There's
little point in refusing—it's booked and paid-for
already.'

Her eyes narrowed, but she unclicked her seatbelt and minutes later they emerged into the crisp,
cold dusk. The streets were adorned by spectacular Christmas lights that arched over them in a
glittering extravagant swirl of stars and planets.

Etta exhaled on a gasp of wonder. 'It's incredible. Every year I forget how fantastic it is.'

Every tree was festooned with brightly lit baubles. The smell of roast chestnuts mingled with

the aroma of mince pies, and a group of teenage carol singers tinged the air with festive songs.

As they joined the bustling throng of Christmas shoppers Etta paused outside each shop window. Every single one was filled with a different festive theme. One designer shop was festooned with greenery and foliage, and enormous red bows, and another was more minimalist, with hundreds of square white presents dangled in an eye-catching concentric design. Another boasted a tableau of angels and cherubs…another depicted an incredible 'partridge in a pear tree' ensemble, made up of different fabrics and beads. But Gabe derived more pleasure from the intent look on Etta's face, as if she were taking mental photographs of each window.

They approached the hotel, where eight abundantly lit gold Christmas trees filled the balustrade above the entrance. The windows blazed and sparkled with strings of dazzling lights, and liveried hotel staff waited to usher them through the ornate revolving doors and into the foyer.

Etta stood stock-still as she gazed at the Christmas tree inside, and Gabe didn't blame her. The enormous realistic-looking spruce was placed in the middle of a carousel straight from Victorian times. Each brightly painted horse seemed to have a character of its own, and each one some-how gave an illusion of movement. The tree itself towered over the signature sweep of the hotel's grand staircase. Hundreds of blown glass orna-ments rested amid the branches, and as he stepped closer Gabe could see that each one depicted an aspect of a funfair: a stick of candy floss, a wind-mill, a toffee apple, a hoopla ring…

Next to him, Etta stirred herself out of her trance. 'Awesome. I could stand and stare at it for hours.'

'And you can. But let's check in first.'

They walked across the marbled floor to the impressive long reception desk.

'Hi. I have a booking under the name of Der-went for a suite with two interconnecting rooms.'

'Yes, I have that right here.'

A bellboy hovered, took their bags and led them to the state-of-the-art lifts. He escorted them up to the eighth floor and opened the door of the suite.

'I've got it from here,' Gabe said, and waited until the youngster had gone before he took Etta through.

Etta stepped into the enormous, beautifully fur-nished room and stopped. 'This is amazing, but it isn't necessary. You didn't need to book a suite.'

'It's safer. My guess is that Tommy will head

down to the Manor, but if he has tracked you to here I'll feel better able to control the situation in a suite.'

'But… I…' Genuine worry creased her features into a frown.

'I really don't understand the problem. I can afford this.' Impatience warred with the novelty of an implied accusation from a woman that he was spending too much on her.

'I understand that, and I don't want to seem ungrateful, but this morning at the press conference you waxed lyrical about Derwent Manor and your family, and your commitment to raising money for its maintenance. That's what the Christmas Fair is about. Yet here you are, squandering Derwent money on this hotel when we could easily have stayed somewhere else at a fraction of the price. I understand that you work for the estate, but I don't see how you can justify your lifestyle with your commitment to maintaining the manor.'

'I'm not "squandering Derwent money".' Gabe exhaled a sigh, irritated to find that the judgement in Etta's tawny eyes had touched a nerve. 'I don't draw my money from the Derwent Estate. I have my own investment business.' He'd decided long ago that he needed independence from his parents, and it turned out he had a real financial flair. 'The money I earn from that funds my lifestyle.'

'Oh.'

There was no mistaking her surprise—in fact her jaw had headed floorward and he gave a rueful twisted smile.

Her tawny brown eyes, soft with contrition, held his as she stepped towards him. 'I'm sorry. I made a judgement based on insufficient evidence. I had you down as nothing but a shallow playboy, living off Daddy's money. Turns out that wasn't the full picture.'

Now she was closer, and one small hand reached up and rested on his forearm. The touch fizzed against the cotton of his shirt. The moment stretched, the scent of strawberry shampoo assailed his nostrils, and as she looked up at him, then closed the gap between them, the urge to kiss those full lush lips nearly overwhelmed him. The approval in her eyes warmed his skin and a warning flare was set off in his brain.

He did not need Etta Mason's *approval*. Annoyance banded his chest. There had been no need to tell her about his company, to volunteer information. As for the urge to kiss her—he'd be damned if he did. Etta had made it clear their mutual attraction was not welcome and he would respect that—wouldn't risk spooking her. Not when the new family tree was on the line. The ball was in her court—it was her choice what to do with it.

Stepping back, he kept his voice light. 'Well, now you know. I'm a shallow playboy living off my own money.' Another step back and he glanced at his watch. 'Our table is booked in an hour, so I'll meet you back here then.'

For a second she stood as if frozen, then one slim hand rose and touched her lips. 'Sounds like a plan.'

Etta practically leapt across the room and dived into her bedroom. The click of the lock turning was more than expressive of her feelings.

CHAPTER SIX

ETTA STARED AT her flushed face in the enormous chrome-framed mirror that reflected a positively palatial art deco bathroom—white sinks embedded in beds of marble, snow-white towels hanging from gleaming heated rails... Somehow she had to get a grip. It was as if the surroundings had somehow turned her light-headed. The surroundings or the man who had provided them.

Enough. She loathed these sensations he induced. Back in that empress-worthy lounge, with its sleek modern furnishings and sumptuous cushioned sofas, she had wanted him to kiss her. *Again.*

Time to take control. No way—*no way*—would she lose her hard-won self-respect and throw herself at Gabriel Derwent. She would *not* give him any vestige of power over her—would not let these giddy feelings sway her, make her take her eye off what was important. She was a professional, a career woman, a renowned historian—not a foolish teenager as she had been with Tommy. When she had allowed feelings and sensations to override all sense and decency.

Never again.

That moment earlier had been an aberration— nothing more. Brought on by the emotional intensity of the past days and by yet another of her misconceptions about Gabriel Derwent being tumbled down. From now on in it would be professional all the way.

One blissful shower later and she gazed at her wardrobe choice, then pulled out a midnight blue fifties-inspired evening dress. Perfect. Long-sleeved, with a straight demure neckline, and a fun flared skirt, cinched at the waist with a vintage belt.

As she buckled her high-heeled Mary Janes her mobile rang.

'Steph. Is everything OK?'

'Everything is fine,' her best friend said cheerfully. 'Ethan got us here safely. No sign of Tommy and the cruise ship is awesome. The girls are in seventh heaven and I'm about to embark on a cocktail. So don't worry about anything.'

Ten minutes later Etta dropped her phone into her vintage evening bag and headed for the lounge. Bracing herself for the inevitable impact, she opened the door and instructed her lungs to breathe.

Gabe stood by an enormous arched window against the magically lit backdrop of Mayfair. His blond hair glistened with the remnants of a shower, and she stood mesmerised as he shrugged a dark grey jacket over a pristine white shirt. The expensive material seemed to mould to the breadth of his shoulders and she gulped. Without her brain's permission her gaze dropped to the triangle of skin at the apex of his chest and a small shiver ran through her.

For a crazy moment she didn't care about self-respect or professionalism. She wanted to walk across the room and press her finger over that patch of bare skin.

Well, tough. That wasn't happening.

As he turned she forced her features into neutral and fixed a cool smile to her lips. There was a silence, and then, his jaw clenched, he stepped forward. 'Let's go,' he said.

'Right behind you.'

And what a view that is, whispered a small, defiant unprofessional part of her as they descended the grand staircase.

The hotel glowed with a mingling of wealth and Christmas cheer, and the sheer decadence of the art deco foyer was completed with a chandelier that threw out beams of diamond-white light that played and sparkled over the wreath-laden walls.

Lights and baubles arched over the entrances, fluted pillars trailed tiny iridescent lights, and floral displays spread their magnificence over glass-topped tables and filled the air with heavenly scents. Just for a moment Etta relaxed, almost wishing this were a real date. *Almost.* After all, her track record with dates was hardly stellar.

They walked towards the entrance to the restaurant—a curtained doorway that rippled with a dark green tasselled fabric. Etta stepped through and gasped...

The vast vaulted ceiling gave the room an organic simple feel, and the predominant colours of green and brown gave the area an enchanted sylvan warmth. Walnut tables with slate placemats dotted the floor around the centrepiece—a bare-branched tree with stars hanging from every polished wooden limb.

'This is fabulous,' she said as a waiter led them to their table.

As they walked she became aware of the looks directed at them—or rather at Gabe—and her step faltered slightly, though he seemed oblivious.

'Is it difficult?' she asked, once they were seated on green leather chairs.

'What?'

'Being recognised all the time?'

'You get used to it. My parents always taught Kaitlin and me to use the attention if we could, but also always to be aware of how our behaviour could impact upon the family image.'

'What about Cora?'

'Cora pretty much avoided *any* publicity—even as a child. My parents had to focus on Kaitlin and me as Derwent ambassadors.'

'I'm with Cora on that one.' Etta glanced swiftly around and resisted the urge to wriggle in her seat. 'What about *my* behaviour? If I eat with the wrong knife will that impact on you?'

'You're looking at it the wrong way. You should be thinking how to use the situation to your advantage. Most women do.'

'Isn't that a bit cynical?'

Etta studied the menu. Her tastebuds cartwheeled, already jumping about in anticipation as she read the selection. Each item was a seasonal delicacy that offered local fresh produce with a twist.

'No. It's the truth. But I don't mind if my date

can score a bit of beneficial publicity—good for her. As long as she doesn't lie or smear me in any way, I don't begrudge her.'

No wonder he'd assumed she would jump at the chance to pose as his girlfriend. 'Well, I don't want to exploit your name or your title. In any way. In fact I hope that the press were thoroughly diverted from the scent this morning. If April Fotherington saw us here she would *definitely* get the wrong end of the stick.' The reporter was renowned for her ability to track down celebrities and unearth the juiciest of stories. 'She has pulled off some pretty big celebrity scoops.'

Amusement gleamed in his eyes. 'So you're a celebrity gossip magazine reader?'

'I'm not. Well, I am—but only because of Steph. She reads them avidly and I end up browsing through them too.'

'You two are really close?'

'Yup. Steph is like family.' Her mind flashed to the birth parents she'd never known, to the adoptive parents who were now lost to her, and to the younger sister she'd barely got a chance to know. *Close it down.* 'Like an older sister, really.'

'How did you meet?'

'At a mother and baby music class when Cathy

and Martha were small. The rest of the group didn't exactly approve of me—I was a seventeen-year-old with a toddler. But Steph looked out for me. Actually bothered to talk to me. If it hadn't been for her I'd have cut and run. Anyway, Steph was a single mum too—she'd adopted Martha after her marriage broke down.'

That was another reason why they had connected. Steph had shown Etta that adoption could be a *good* thing—her relationship with Martha was honest, open, and full of love.

'She's ten years older than me but we clicked, and Martha and Cathy bonded instantly, so our friendship took off from there.'

'You're lucky to have each other.'

'I know. We are totally different, but it doesn't seem to matter. Steph would love all this.' Etta glanced round the room. 'She'd agree with you that I should take complete advantage of you.'

Oh, hell. Had she said that? The words took on a double meaning that she hadn't planned, and now the words kept tumbling out.

'I mean…I mean she thought I should take you up on the girlfriend idea and enjoy the publicity and the dinners and a romantic getaway. A *fake* romantic getaway obviously.'

Stop the talk. Now.

'I've told you it's not too late to change your mind.'

Lazy amusement touched his voice and she narrowed her eyes. No way would she let him think she regretted her decision.

'The ball's in your court,' he continued.

'That's where it's staying.' Yet her tummy did a loop-the-loop at the depth of his voice, the way his dark eyes rested on her lips. 'I was talking about *Steph*, and as I said she and I are chalk and cheese.'

'So Steph would go for the shallow playboy type?'

'Yes.'

'But you won't because…? Remind me again.'

'Because there is more to attraction than the physical side of things.'

Really? asked her sceptical hormones—after all, in the last few years there had been no 'physical side' at all. With anyone. Just a sad series of failed fizz-free dates that had culminated in nothing. And before that there had been a couple of tepid relationships that were best consigned to the 'bedroom disaster' category of her memory banks.

'So you admit there *is* a physical attraction?'

'I…' Darn the man! 'That is irrelevant.'

'It seems pretty relevant to me.'

'I said there has to be *more* than physical appeal.'

'Sure—I agree. Conversation is useful too. You and I don't seem to have any problem there.'

'That is still not enough.'

'It works for me. What's wrong with a few days of fun, no strings attached?'

'It's just *wrong.*'

The idea of letting go, revelling in sensation, was impossible to imagine.

An echo of her mum came: *'Never cross the line, Etta.'* Any line. Even the smallest of childhood fibs had been a heinous crime. Her first Valentine, when she'd been aged ten—an innocent offering—had drawn forth horror. Her parents had made her tear it up into little pieces and told her she must have behaved with 'promiscuity' to attract it. She'd had to look the word up in a dictionary, and even now the remembered burn of shame seared her soul. Even though she'd come to understand her parents' actions—they had been on a constant lookout for her unknown genes to show themselves.

'So you disapprove from a *moral* viewpoint? You shouldn't.' The amusement had vanished now and his voice was edged with cold. 'I am still in touch with nearly all the women I've dated. They aren't mindless bimbos. They are all passionate and fun-loving and we had good times—in bed and out. They did nothing *wrong* and neither did I.'

'I understand that, and I *don't* disapprove. It just doesn't make sense to me. What's the point of entering into a short-term relationship with no future?'

'That's like saying, "What's the point of going to a party?" just because you know it will end.'

'You can't equate a party to a relationship.'

'Why not?' His mouth quirked up, and the teasing glint was back in his blue-grey eyes.

'Because a party is a social gathering and a relationship is a…a connection between two people.'

'Exactly—and those two people can define that connection in whatever way they want. They can make an agreement, an alliance, a pact to last a few days or a lifetime. You scratch my back, or whatever bit you choose, and I'll scratch yours.'

Her back positively tingled in response, and her tummy turned to hot, gooey mush at the thought. His smile expanded and a wave of relief washed over her at the arrival of the waiter with their entrées.

As she thanked him, and inhaled the exquisite

aromas that arose from her plate, she gathered her thoughts. She would not back down on this. Would not let the ledge of certainty she'd always camped out on crumble.

'Nope. You've got it wrong. Relationships *can't* be a pact because relationships involve emotions and you can't control those or agree on them. Emotions don't remain static. You may enter into the pact with the best intentions, but feelings could develop. How do you know you won't fall in love with one of these short-term women or vice versa?'

Ha. Etta forked up a mouthful of her starter and exhaled a small huff of pleasure. The seared venison had a smoky juniper taste, and the tang of elderberries and the crunch of walnuts in the salad made her savour each bite.

Gabe took a sip of wine. 'So you wouldn't have a fling with me because you're worried you'd fall in love with me or I'd fall in love with you?'

'*No!* Because neither of those things would happen.'

'Exactly. So what's the problem?'

Etta narrowed her eyes. 'We are talking in general. *I* wouldn't have a fling with you because you are not my type.'

'Oh, yes. I'd forgotten.'

The drawl was underlain with a molten heat that warmed her skin.

But she would not succumb to attraction or distraction. 'You haven't answered the question. How do you know one or the other of you won't fall in love?'

'The time frame, for one. I keep my flings short. And I'm very clear upfront about the terms of agreement. The only thing on offer is short-term fun—love is not on the table and neither is my title.'

'So you aren't planning on marriage?'

That didn't make sense. Surely the future Duke of Fairfax had to get married in order to ensure the continuity of the line.

'Not with someone who isn't within my social circle.'

Outrage rendered her near speechless and she could only gawp at him as the waiter cleared their plates and served them their main course. '*Excuse me?* So you believe all these wonderful, liberated women of yours…are *beneath* you? That they aren't worthy to be the Duchess of Fairfax?'

An answering streak of anger flashed lightning-like in his stormcloud-grey eyes and Etta was aware of a strange exhilaration.

'That is not what I said. You're a historian.

Haven't farmers and shepherds always wanted to marry farmers' daughters? Women who understand the truth of farming—the back-breaking labour, the weather, the hours, and the work. Or do they want to marry someone who thinks farming is all about sweet little lambs?'

'So you're saying us common people think being a duchess is all about wearing a tiara and going to balls, and a true aristocrat knows it's more than that?'

'Something like that. Marriage is an alliance, and I need to ally myself with a woman who will understand what Derwent Manor means to me— who won't see the house as a money-eating pile better given over to a heritage trust. A woman who will enter into a life dedicated to fundraising and ensuring Derwent Manor remains in the family.'

His large hand reached for his wine glass and for a second his eyes dropped to the amber liquid. His lips set in a grim line, as if the idea filled him with bleak rather than happy thoughts.

'And you think a "commoner" won't be up to the job.'

'Don't twist my words. I just think it would be *easier* for someone used to it. And it will make everyone's life easier if I marry someone who will get on with my parents. Someone who fits.'

'So you're marrying to please your parents?' That seemed impossible to believe of a man of his strength.

'No. But I can't see the harm in marrying someone they approve of.'

A funny little pang assaulted Etta—that ruled her *right* out, then.

'It will lessen the chances of adverse publicity and make working together easier. I'm all for an easy life.'

'What about love?'

Gabe shook his head. 'Love isn't in the equation. It's not a factor. It's not on the table because I neither require love nor offer it. I believe my alliance is more likely to endure without it. Bottom line, love is not relevant.'

She couldn't help but wonder why he believed that. Of course he needed to marry—she understood that—but it all sounded so clinical. Presumably the Duke and Duchess had made an 'alliance', and expected their son and heir to do the same. Yet Gabriel wouldn't bow to their wishes if he didn't want to—ergo, he was more than happy to comply. And yet...

'Is this what you *want*, though? A cold-blooded

alliance? It seems a far cry from "having fun, enjoying yourself, no strings attached". What about liking and physical attraction and warm, passionate women?'

'Of course liking is important, and so is physical attraction. But long-term I need someone who shares my goals and understands that there is more to life than my "shallow playboy" existence. So I'll be offering something different to my wife and expecting something different from what I get from my flings.'

'But…' It still seemed wrong.

Leaning over, he topped up their wine glasses. 'Enough of my attitude to love and marriage,' he said. 'What about yours?'

Etta took a sip of the golden liquid with its overtones of elderflower and narrowed her eyes. *Botheration!* The last thing she wanted was to discuss her inadequacy, her missing gene, her inability to connect romantically. Yet she'd sat here and interrogated Gabe on *his* attitude to love without compunction. Fair was fair.

CHAPTER SEVEN

GABE CRADLED HIS wine glass, watched the swirl of emotions crossing Etta's face—the crease of her brow, the angle of her cheekbone, the quick gesture to tuck a tendril of chestnut hair behind her ear—and wondered how a business dinner had morphed into this. Perhaps he should shut this down now, but he didn't want to—he welcomed the distraction from his own thoughts and the prospect of his marriage.

It was a merger that would now have a key component missing. Children. His hopes and expectations had dissipated to dust, but marriage was still a necessity. The manor would need a duchess and if—no, *when*—he found another heir, that man's wife would need a role model. Because Gabe had every intent of persuading this heir to take his duties and responsibilities seriously; he owed it to his name, to the estate, to find a way forward. But tonight he wanted to forget that.

'When you're ready.'

Her shoulders lifted. 'My attitude to love and marriage is easy enough to encapsulate. They aren't for me.'

'Why not?' Surprise made him raise his eyebrows—somehow he'd expected someone as vital as Etta Mason to embrace love. Assumed her antipathy to a short-term fling sprang from a desire for a waltz over the happy-ever-after horizon.

'I'm not made that way. I'm truly happier on my own. I'm in charge—I don't have to ask anyone's permission or compromise in any way at all. If I want to get home and change into my PJs, curl up on the sofa and watch a history film and eat cereal I can.'

'So you're choosing sugar-coated flakes over sex, love, and companionship?'

'No! I'm choosing independence and being happy on my own over the pointless pursuit of romance.'

'How can you know it's pointless?'

'Because I've tried. For a while I felt that I needed to find a man and marry him for Cathy's sake, so she could have a dad. But then I realised that wouldn't be fair to anyone. Most of all me. I prefer to be on my own. I've done just fine without a man in my life.'

As if realising she might be protesting too much,

she sat back and then picked up her knife and fork to pierce her last piece of fish.

'Maybe you haven't met the right man yet. Every man isn't a Tommy.'

'I *know* that. This is nothing to do with Tommy. I know most men are decent individuals. I *liked* a lot of my dates—I'm still friends with a couple of them and I happily danced at their weddings. But romance isn't my thing and I'm OK with that. I like my independence.'

'I get that, but…' But he couldn't help but wonder if, for Etta, independence equalled safety, and whether her willingness to give up on all aspects of a relationship was due to the damage Tommy had inflicted.

'But what?'

There was pride in her voice, as if she dared him to pity her.

'I think it's a waste. I think you're missing out. You've decided against long *and* short-term relationships.'

'I haven't decided anything. It's just how the custard cream has crumbled.'

'Maybe because you're dating the wrong type of guy?'

'So let me guess… You think I should be dating a guy like *you*?'

Gabe shrugged. 'Why not? If romance isn't for you maybe you should consider what someone *like me* can offer. Instead of dating the type of guys you think you *should* be with.'

The words rang across the table and she flinched. 'I do not want what you can offer. Anyway, what's wrong with dating suitable guys? This coming from a man on the lookout for a "suitable" wife.'

'That's different. You've stopped looking—you've given up. I don't want love, but I'm still up for sex and companionship.'

'Well, I don't need those either. From anyone.' Reaching for her glass, she lifted it and took a gulp of wine, placed the crystal flute down and exhaled on a sigh. 'This isn't a topic I want to discuss.' Her words dripped ice. 'Perhaps we could make this business dinner a tad more business-like.'

Good job, Gabe. Slow hand-clap, please.

Etta's love life was *zip* to do with him—so why was he rocking the boat when he needed her on board. He cut a piece of tender fillet steak, alongside some of the buttery, floury potato terrine and balanced the forkful on the edge of his plate.

'So let's talk business.'

* * *

Business. Business, business, *business*. The by-word, the watchword—the *only* word.

It was a mantra Etta repeated to herself every waking second the following day, until they drew up outside the imposing exterior of Derwent Manor. Relief washed over her—now she could get to work, down to *business*, and forget the stupid conversation of the previous night.

Mortification mixed with sheer horror—she'd pretty much admitted to a physical attraction, had laid out the sorry state of her love-life and witnessed his reaction: shock mixed with compassion. With a dose of psychoanalysis. *If romance isn't for you maybe you should consider what someone* like me *can offer. Instead of dating the type of guys you think you* should *be with.*

The words had stung then and the memory of them stung now. The smarting was worsened by a trickle of temptation to cross that line and succumb to their attraction. Become one of those liberated, passionate, and warm women he'd waxed so lyrical about.

Enough. *Business.* No more personal conversations or even thoughts. To be on the safe side she'd requested breakfast in her room and had feigned sleep for the entire journey to Derwent Manor.

Now, as she faked a yawn, she gazed at the manor and nearly choked—of course she'd seen pictures, but nothing could have prepared her for the sheer grandeur of the Elizabethan-style building. The turreted, many-windowed stone building was immense, on a way more opulent scale than the word *manor* suggested.

'It's so big!'

'There was a manor on this site as far back as the thirteenth century, but the building was pretty much scrapped and rebuilt in 1590. It took eight years and who knows how much money. Then in Victorian times it had another makeover—thanks to the Duke at the time cashing in on various industrial schemes. Nowadays we live in some of it, display other rooms to the public and desperately try to pay the maintenance. Kaitlin, Cora, and I used to picture the house actually *eating* money.'

Etta tried to imagine the heating bills, the maintenance costs, and quite simply couldn't. No wonder the Derwents had to dedicate their lives to raising money.

'What do you want to do first?' Gabe asked. 'I could give you a tour, or…'

Etta opened the car door. 'Actually, I'd like to get started. So if you can show me to the records room that would be fantastic.'

Ten minutes later Etta surveyed a room piled with dusty tomes. Shelves adorned the walls and humidifiers stood in two of the corners. An enormous ornate desk was tucked into another corner, stacked with piles of papers and old photo albums.

'I think this is what is known as one damp mess,' Gabe said.

'To me it's like a treasure trove, waiting to be opened. So if it's OK with you I'll get stuck in.'

'Not until we discuss some security measures. By now Tommy will know you're here. Press coverage wasn't huge, but there was an online article saying that I'd hired you and a bit about the fair—he may well have read it.'

Her anticipation at the prospect of losing herself in the fascination of the past came up against the reality of the present, and fear shivered through her. Tommy was going to be livid when he realised Cathy wasn't with her, and the thought of his anger unearthed a swathe of memories. The thud of her heart, the futile entreaties, the pathetic ways she had tried to appease him.

Gabe muttered an expletive under his breath, stepped forward, and encased her hands in his.

Etta allowed herself one brief instant of reassurance and then pulled away as the feeling of reassurance turned to something else—a heat, an awareness of the feel of his skin against hers...

Business. 'I'm sorry. I'm fine.'

'This room is safe, and it doesn't lead directly onto the grounds. Here.'

Automatically Etta stretched out a hand and he placed a white box in her palm.

'It's a panic pendant. You press the button and an alarm runs to my phone.'

'Thank you.'

Yet even as she looped the pendant over her head Etta knew she must not become dependent on Gabriel—must work out a strategy to be rid of Tommy herself. Because once the job was done Gabe's bodyguard duties would cease.

But right now she was safe, and there was a project to embark on. 'Right. I'm going to get started.'

The hours passed by in a welcome blur. A part of her was aware of Gabe's presence, but he didn't interfere as she inspected and stacked and sorted and dusted and felt the comfort of centuries of history envelop her. As she sifted through the records she could almost *feel* the people in them starting to come alive in her mind.

Until... 'Etta. I think you need to stop before you collapse.'

She rose to her feet from where she'd been inspecting a tottering pile of ancient-looking papers and wiped a hand across her forehead. 'What time is it?'

'Dinner time.' Gabe pointed at a plate of now rather limp-looking sandwiches. 'Especially as you haven't touched lunch.'

'I did mean to eat them. I'm sorry. I got completely absorbed.'

'So I can see. But I'm making an executive decision. You need to stop. I haven't even shown you where you're going to sleep. So, come on, I'll show you your room, then you can freshen up and give me a progress report over dinner.'

'OK.' Etta looked down at herself and grimaced. *Filthy* didn't quite cover it.

As she followed Gabe out of the records room and down a long corridor she took in the faint air of dinginess in the peeling wallpaper and the slight smell of must and damp. Then Gabe pushed a door open and Etta blinked.

'This part of the house is open to the public,' he said.

The contrast was marked: a gleaming oak staircase curved upwards with imposing elegance, polished furniture from times gone by sat on shiny wooden flooring, and gilt-edged portraits adorned the walls.

Etta trailed her hand along the carved oak as she mounted the richly carpeted stairs, and peeped into rooms resplendent with tapestries and velvet and history.

'Here we are.' Gabe unlocked a door marked Private and they stepped through into a shabby hallway. 'All our money is poured into the upkeep of the estate and the public areas of the house. So I'm afraid you won't be staying in historic splendour yourself.'

'These rooms are still part of history. I'm guessing they were the servants' quarters... Perhaps one of my ancestors worked as a scullery maid here.'

Gabriel pushed a door open. 'Hopefully you'll be fairly comfortable in here.'

'Of course I will.'

The room was simply furnished, but it was clean, and although the walls could have done with a coat of paint there were fresh flowers on the dresser and the eaves and cornices were a reminder of ages past.

'I'll knock for you in half an hour. The bathroom is across the hall.'

* * *

Half an hour later Gabe watched Etta seat herself at the large wooden table in the airy well-equipped kitchen. She was dressed in jeans and an oversized jumper, her chestnut hair hung in damp tendrils round her make-up-free face, and she looked absurdly young.

She inhaled appreciatively as Gabriel ladled beef casserole onto a pile of wild rice and handed her the plate. 'This smells divine. Did you make it?'

'Not me. I can cook, but not to this standard. Our housekeeper made it. Sarah has been here for years, and she is always thrilled when one of us comes back to stay.'

In truth, Sarah had been one of the people he'd missed most when he'd been at boarding school. She was one of the few people who had ever hugged the Derwent children.

'So you don't live here?'

'No. I've got my own place in London.' One day, when he married, he planned to renovate one of the old empty houses on the estate. No way would he expect his wife to live with his parents in the manor, however suitable she might be. No way could *he* live with his parents—the idea was impossible to picture.

'It must have been amazing to grow up here. I felt thrilled for Cathy when I got us a place with a tiny patch of lawn and her own bedroom. So all this space and the gardens... It must have been magical.'

'I didn't really spend that much time here.' He kept his voice deliberately even.

Etta's forehead creased. 'Where were you? I thought the Derwents lived here pretty much all year round?'

'I went to boarding school at eight and I spent a lot of the holidays at various camps.'

Camps to toughen him up. His parents had been appalled when their son and heir had run away from boarding school. His gut still twisted when he remembered the first step in their 'toughen up Gabe' regime—they had sacked his nanny, who had also looked after Kaitlin and Cora.

In truth Megan Anstey had been more of a mother to him than the Duchess had ever been, and he could still taste the grief, feel the tears pounding the back of his eyelids. Tears he'd held in because he'd known if he'd cried his parents would blame Megan, would hold back her references. So he'd uttered a polite, formal goodbye, and later that afternoon he'd been driven back to boarding school.

The entire journey was etched on his memory. Suppressed tears, the tang of grief at the loss of Megan, and the pang of guilt at the consequences to Megan of *his* actions. The realisation had come that if he hadn't let Megan close then he wouldn't be feeling this pain and neither would she.

Then, as the car had sped over the country roads, he had felt the clench of fear in his gut at the knowledge of what awaited him: the glee-edged cruelty and ritual persecution from the bullies. He'd loathed himself for the sheer helplessness he'd felt. Had made a decision that his parents were right—his only option was to toughen up. One day he would make up for his error to Megan Anstey, but he wouldn't let her or anyone else close again. And one day he would take on the bullies and he would win.

Both those days had been a long time coming, but one of his first acts when he'd had money of his own had been to track Megan down and give her a substantial cheque. As for the bullies—eventually he'd got tough enough to fight.

'Oh.' Etta's delicate features were scrunched into an expression of perplexity. 'I can't imagine how that must have felt. I don't think I could have sent Cathy away, missed so much of her childhood.'

'*All* the male Derwents go to boarding school.' Though he had vowed with intensity that he would never send a child of *his* away. Though now that wouldn't be an issue. In any sense of the word. The now familiar ache tightened his chest.

'That must have been tough on your mother.'

He doubted that—his parents had been remote figures all his life. Oh, he knew they were proud of him—proud of his looks and charisma, proud to have produced a healthy male heir. But they had barely registered his absence as a person.

'Did you want to go?' Etta asked, her eyes wide with a mix of curiosity and sympathy.

It was impossible to lie—not when he remembered the bleak horror of those first years. Until he'd learnt to fight back, form alliances, and never show weakness.

'I accepted it,' he stated flatly.

'That doesn't answer—' She broke off as the doorbell rang: a hard, insistent peal. One slender hand rose and rubbed her chest, as if fear had clasped her heart. 'Tommy…' she whispered.

CHAPTER EIGHT

GABE ROSE TO his feet. 'Wait here.'

The temptation to do just that showed on her face, but then she shook her head and pushed back her chair. 'If it's Tommy it's my problem. You're here to guard me. I'm supposed to deal with him.'

Admiration surged inside him—Etta was whiter than milk, and he could see the fear in her eyes, but her back was ramrod-straight as she moved from behind the table.

'All right. But remember if it *is* Tommy I will not let him hurt you. OK?'

A slight hint of colour returned to her cheeks. 'OK,' she repeated as the doorbell rang out again in staccato buzzes. 'But be careful.'

'I will be.' Gabe smiled as an adrenaline buzz kicked into his veins.

They walked through the kitchen and down the corridor to the front door. Gabe tugged it open, unsurprised to see Tommy slouched against the jamb, dressed in jeans and a leather jacket. The dark-haired man smiled—a slow sneer—and Gabe tensed, ready to push Etta behind him.

'Where's my daughter?'

'Not here.' Etta's voice was breathy but clear.

'Then where *is* she? We need to discuss this, Etta. Cathy is my daughter too.'

'There is nothing to discuss.'

'But there is, darlin', there *is*. I've talked to a lawyer and now I want to talk to you. You know it's better to give me what I want.'

Etta flinched, then nodded. 'Ten minutes. We're in the middle of dinner.'

Gabe led the way into a small anteroom.

'Dinner?' Tommy said. 'Very cosy.' His dark blue eyes darted between Etta and Gabe. 'Guess she hasn't got you between the sheets yet, then?'

'Enough.' Gabe moved forward and in one seamless move slammed Tommy against the wall. He saw the surprise in the other man's eyes and revelled in it. 'Let's keep this clean, shall we? Say what you need to say and get out.'

He released his grasp and for a second he thought the other man would go for him—he saw the malevolent gleam in his eye. *Bring it on.*

But then Tommy shrugged, walked over to a chair, and sprawled in it. 'I want to speak to you alone, Etta.'

'No.' Etta folded her arms across her chest. 'Whatever you need to say you can say it in front of Gabe.'

'Whatever?' The word dripped with malice. 'Perhaps we can take a trip down memory lane? I can tell the toff *exactly* what you like and the best way to make you listen.'

Against all probability Etta's complexion took on an even deeper pallor.

'If that's how you want to spend your ten minutes, feel free. But the clock's ticking, Tommy,' Gabe told him.

'Say what you need to say.' Etta's voice was low, but steady, and Gabe hoped the reminder of his presence had helped. 'I've consulted a lawyer too. You're not on the birth certificate. You have no parental responsibility.'

'But I can apply for a court order. Or… Cathy is sixteen- if she wanted she could even move in with me.'

'She'd need my consent until she was eighteen.'

'That's a technicality and you know it. I think in real life there won't be anything you can do about it.' Tommy smiled and settled back in the chair. 'You know I always hated the idea of a family, but now I'm thinking maybe I was wrong. I *like* the idea of having a daughter—someone who carries my blood, my genes—and I believe I have the right to be part of her life. Teach her my ways and my beliefs. You took that opportunity from me, Etta—you ran away and you took away my chance to be a dad.'

'You didn't *want* to be a father.' Etta's voice was tight, and her hands rubbed up and down her arms. 'You punched me in the stomach to try and get rid of the baby.'

Gabe's blood chilled and he stepped forward even as Tommy shook his head. 'That was *your* fault, Etta. You defied me and you know I don't like that. That's something Cathy will need to learn too. It's something I had to learn from *my* father, and it's a tough lesson but an important one.' He rose to his feet. 'Of course I would never hurt Cathy—I'm a reformed man. You see how I didn't lay a finger on your toff, here. I came because I want to give you a heads-up. Let you know I'm coming after my daughter. You took her from me once—now it's my turn. You and me…we've unfinished business. I owe you, and another thing my old man taught me is to always pay my debts.'

Etta stood as if rooted to the spot, her tawny eyes shocked, and anger made Gabe's fists clench. 'You've said your piece. I'll see you out.'

As he walked Tommy to the door Gabe held

tight to his anger—yes, his foot itched to boot the man as far as he could kick him, but that wouldn't help the situation.

'Don't come back.'

Gabe shut and locked the door and made his way back to the kitchen. Etta was standing exactly where he'd left her, his arms wrapped around her body, shivering, her lip caught between her teeth.

'He's gone.' Gabe moved towards her. 'Come into the lounge. I'll light a fire and get us a drink.'

Ten minutes later he rose from the fireplace as the logs caught and the flames crackled into a blaze. The scent of pine invaded the air and Etta released a small sigh, as if the warmth gave her comfort. Gabe strode to the lacquered drinks cabinet, selected a bottle of cognac and poured a generous measure into two balloon glasses.

'Here.'

Etta reached up from the depths of the armchair she had curled into. 'Thank you.'

'You're still shivering.' Gabe pulled his thick knitted jumper over his head and handed it to her. 'Put this on until the fire kicks in.'

A hesitation, and then she accepted it. 'Sorry. Tommy really spooked me this time.'

'No need to apologise. The man is clearly, as you said, a first-class nutter and downright scary. I'm sorry you ever hooked up with him—it must have been hell.' The memory of her words, the revelation of how he had hurt her, still iced his veins, made him want to force Tommy to his knees to grovel before her.

'It was.' The words were simple. 'But I'm glad he came here today.' She straightened up and tugged at the sleeves of his jumper so she could pick up her glass. 'Because it's made my decision. I know how I'll deal with Tommy.'

'How?'

'Exactly how I did sixteen years ago. I'm going to run—take Cathy and disappear.'

'Or you could stand your ground.'

'I can't fight him. You saw it for yourself—he's a nutter. No amount of restraining orders will stop him—even if I could get one. I won't risk Cathy, and it won't be for ever. Tommy is a criminal, through and through. All I have to do is run until he gets himself put behind bars again. Cathy and I can take off—go backpacking somewhere or relocate for a while.'

'And then what? What happens when he gets out of prison the next time?'

'I'll deal with that when it happens.'

'No.'

Gabe realised he'd said the word with way more

force than he'd intended. But he knew that this was not the way to deal with a man like Tommy—with any bully. He had first-hand experience, and as an adult he'd done enough work with children—both bullies *and* the bullied—to know that running away, showing fear, kept the cycle going.

'It won't work. I get that you're scared, but running will make Tommy worse. He relishes your fear. He didn't need to come here today, or stalk you to Cornwall. If this was only about Cathy he'd contact her. This is about making you suffer.'

'Well, he's good at that.' The bitter undertone spoke volumes about her bleak memories. 'But I don't care about me. It's Cathy I'm scared for. And that's why I'll run. To keep her safe.'

'You don't have to do that. Not when you've worked so hard to get where you are. Don't throw it all away.'

'I won't. I'll just be putting it aside for a while. You don't get it, Gabe. None of it matters more than Cathy.'

'There *is* an alternative.'

'What? I kill him? Tempting, but unfortunately not feasible.'

'Call his bluff. I don't think he has any interest in Cathy—he just wants to punish *you*. Let Tommy see Cathy.'

'Excuse me?' Etta thunked her glass down on the side table, the expression in her tawny eyes morphing from incredulity to anger.

'I don't mean hand her over. I mean set up a supervised meeting. From what I saw of her, it seems to me that Cathy is a strong, intelligent girl. And that you and she have a strong bond.'

For a moment envy touched him as he tried to imagine his own parents forging any bond with their children except one of duty. He remembered the photos on Steph's walls, depicting the years of Cathy and Martha's childhood.

'Am I right?'

'Yes.' Etta's expression softened. 'Cathy has some teenage moments, but she has got a great outlook on life. She worked hard, got excellent GCSEs, and she has a plan for her future, great friends. That's the point. I won't let Tommy ruin that.'

'Then maybe you should trust her. And yourself. You've brought up a very together, bright young woman. Trust her to see Tommy for what he is. Then he loses his power over you.'

For a scant second she considered his words as she swirled the cognac round the glass and watched the dark golden ripples. Then she shook her head. 'You don't understand. You *can't* understand. You are Gabriel Derwent, Earl of Wycliffe, one day the Duke of Fairfax. You have a long line of ancestors at your back, two parents, two siblings—a whole family tree. Cathy has *me*. I'm her entire family tree. So of course she wants a dad.'

'It doesn't always work like that.' Gabe figured that one mum like Etta completely topped two parents like the Duke and Duchess in the parenting stakes. 'Cathy won't want a dad like Tommy.'

'Tommy knows how to turn on the charm. I know that all too well. And it's not only that. I'm not excusing any of his behaviour, but he did have a rough time himself—everyone knew that his dad was an evil man who beat up his wife *and* his kids. Tommy got the worst of it—it was like his dad hated him. Cathy will feel instant sympathy for him. I can picture it all now. Tommy will present himself as the reformed convict or the wronged rebel. He'll admit his sins, tell Cathy he wants to make it up to her, and Cathy is susceptible.'

'Maybe so. But Cathy loves you—her bond is with *you*. You won't lose her to Tommy.'

Etta shook her head and the sadness on her face twisted his chest.

'Bonds break, Gabe.'

Her voice vibrated with emotion and Gabe wondered exactly what bonds she meant.

'Especially around me,' she added, so softly he wasn't sure he'd heard the words. 'But you're right. I won't lose Cathy—if I have to run to the ends of the earth, I will.' She lifted her glass to her lips and drained it. Then she rose in one lithe movement. 'Thank you for having my back with Tommy, and thank you for the drink. Now it's business as usual. I'm heading to my room and I'll be back to work first thing.'

Relief that she was backing away from further confidences mingled with his frustration that she would give up her hard-won life. But he had to back off—Etta was not someone who had come to him for advice, not one of the kids he tried to help. She was an adult, and so far she had done fine without him. Yet it took enormous effort to hold himself back from holding forth.

'OK. I'll be next door. Any problems, bang on the wall.'

Two weeks later Etta glared at the wall—exactly as she did every night. Right now she was suffering a veritable *multitude* of problems.

Not so much in the daytime, because then she could throw herself into work. The Derwent family tree fascinated her during waking minutes; the only niggle to her absorption was a nagging feeling that somehow Gabriel was orchestrating her work. There was nothing she could pinpoint as such, and it might well be that her thoughts were skewed by her constant awareness of him. An awareness she loathed for that very reason—it made her lose perspective.

As did her inability to sleep. Every night—every time she closed her eyes—Tommy loomed behind her lids. With every creak she imagined him sneaking through the darkness of the house. Worse, though, were the images of him finding Cathy. In the depth of night the scenario spun out... Tommy getting ever closer to the cruise ship, boarding...

And as each nightmare wove its dark spell the urge to bang on the wall grew ever larger. Stupid, stupid, *stupid*. Every instinct warned Etta that Gabe represented danger—and yet he made her feel safe, and she wanted him to chase away the shadows and the spectres of her imagination.

Not happening.

Instead she would do the mature thing—get up, get dressed, make a soothing cup of herbal tea and get an early start. Especially as she had unearthed some very interesting facts in the past few days.

Five minutes later she tiptoed to the door, holding her breath as she pulled it open.

One step onto the scruffy carpet of the hall and she stopped short as Gabe's door opened and he stepped out. Etta nearly swallowed her tongue. Dark blond hair sleep-tousled, blue-grey eyes fully alert, he pulled a dark grey T-shirt over his head, allowing her a glimpse of the glorious expanse of his chest.

There it was again—that stupid spark that she couldn't seem to douse. Wrenching her eyes from the golden skin, Etta turned away.

'Are you OK?'

Questionable. 'I'm fine. I couldn't sleep, so I thought I'd make myself a cup of herbal tea and start early.'

'OK. Give me a second and I'll come with you. You can give me your daily update early.'

'Sure.'

Etta glanced at him, further convinced that there was something odd about all these updates; they seemed out of character. She'd watched Gabe over the past weeks and the man worked like a demon. But what she had also noted was his ability to *delegate*, not to micromanage but to trust his staff to carry out the tasks necessary to convert the manor into a Victorian Christmas masterpiece.

Yet with the family tree he seemed interested in every minute detail.

Tea in hand, they entered the records room and Gabe pulled a chair up to the desk. Etta braced herself, inhaled the now so familiar tang of citrus soap and pure Gabe—almost as necessary as her first coffee of the morning.

Focus, Etta.

'I've discovered something really interesting. I haven't mentioned it before because I wanted to be sure, and now I am. I've found a whole new branch of the family. It's one I originally thought had died out, but in actual fact this man here—' she pointed at a name '—married again and had a son. Very soon after that he died and his wife remarried. I think everyone must have thought this son was actually from her second marriage, but he wasn't.'

'Are you absolutely sure?'

'Yes. I've done extensive research, and I've got copies of various records. Although he took his stepfather's name, and inherited his property, I'm sure that he actually belongs on the *Derwent* family tree.'

Gabe scanned the enormous rough diagram Etta had put together. 'Looks good.'

'It's better than good.' She tugged a piece of

paper towards her and skimmed her finger down the line of names. 'His line goes all the way to the present. I mean it's pretty convoluted—he's your cousin practically a million times removed, and I doubt he even knows he is even distantly related to you, but he is. Linked directly back to the 5th Duke.'

His body stilled and for a heartbeat a blaze of heat streaked across his eyes, gone so fast she wondered if it had been a mere trick of the light.

'Fascinating,' he stated. 'I've never so much as heard of this branch of the family tree. You're doing a fantastic job. Next I'd like you to follow the branch we discussed yesterday. I want to find out more about my Great-Great-Great-Aunt Josephine—she sounds like a real character.'

'Sure. Anyone who singlehandedly fought off a band of desperate ruffians with a borrowed sword is worth a mention.'

Etta frowned… Had there been a hint of strain in his voice? Plus, surely her discovery warranted a bit more discussion and considerably more interest. By her reckoning, given the intricacies of peerage inheritance laws, this distant cousin could well be next in line to the Dukedom after Gabe. 'Will you do anything about the distant cousin?'

'As you said, it's unlikely he has any idea who

the Derwents are.' Gabe's voice was dismissive. He rose from his chair. 'I wonder if you'd like a break from the family tree today? In your other role as fair consultant I need your help with the Christmas decorations, and you have been holed up in here for days.'

Etta hesitated, sensing his reserve, wondering if she'd hit some sort of nerve. But if she had it clearly wasn't a nerve he wished to discuss. Perhaps her reference to this new branch of his family tree had reminded him of his need to settle down, to abandon his playboy lifestyle and find his suitable wife. Maybe he regretted turning away Lady Isobel...

And maybe this was Gabe's personal business and as such none of hers. 'I'd love to.'

Relief tinged his smile. 'Good. Come with me. I need you to cast an eye over the tree, and also I'm setting up some stalls so people can make their own Victorian wreaths and ornaments...'

It was impossible not to admire the dedication he'd given to tackling the Victorian theme, and admiration filled her at how much he'd achieved in so short a space of time.

As she followed him into the Great Hall she slammed to a stop as she gazed at the Christmas tree and her jaw dropped. She gawped. It was the most enormous spruce she'd ever seen, but what held her speechless were the ornaments that hung from it.

'They aren't actually antique Victorian—they're vintage Victorian-*style*.' Gabe's voice held satisfaction and appreciation. 'But they're beautiful, aren't they?'

Etta stepped forward and gently touched a stunning angel decoration. 'This is incredible…'

The balloon-shaped ornament contained a Victorian-style chromolithographic angel holding a candle. Its lavish trimmings included vintage tinsel ribbon as well as narrow chenille, antique beaded ribbon and more beautiful spun glass. Further up the tree a vintage-style Santa Claus with a frosty glittery beard hung, framed inside a gold paper medallion.

'Forget incredible. Each one is *exquisite*.' She glanced round the room. 'You've outdone yourself.'

He really had. In true Victorian-style greenery abounded—spruce, cedar, ivy and holly was draped and hung and garlanded over the furniture…the walls…the banisters and chandeliers in a beautiful sweeping display. The scent of cedar infused the air and made her tingle with the spirit of Christmas. Garlands of cranberries and popcorn, tinsel and paper chains streamed over the ceilings and coloured glass lamps shone in the darkness of the early December morning.

'The Victorians really did know how to push a whole flotilla of boats out. But I couldn't have done all this without my staff and all the helpers.'

'Too right, Gabe,' came the cheerful tones of a young man who had entered, laden with a basket of logs.

'Sam. How did the match go?'

'We won. It was a hard game, and I got me leg bashed in when a dirty b—' He glanced at Etta and blushed. 'When one of the opponents took me down. But he was too late. I managed to pass the ball, just like you said, and we got the try.'

He deposited the logs by the fireplace and he and Gabe did some sort of complicated high five.

'Oh, and Dad sends his regards and says to tell you that he'll be here early for the fair. He'll set up the lights and then he'll be on standby, and Mum's cooking up a storm.'

'Sounds fabulous. I'll drop in to see them later.'

'Cheers, Gabe. Catch you later.'

It was incredible, really. There was no side at all to Gabe's interaction with his employees—no feeling of a social or class divide other than a difference in accent and no feudal spirit, as such.

And yet she sensed that his employees felt a fierce loyalty to the man who would one day be the Duke of Fairfax.

Everyone was working all-out on the fair—none more so than Gabe—and they worked with an easy camaraderie that indicated a long-term two-way friendship and respect. The kind instigated by a man with integrity and a genuine loyalty to his land—not a shallow playboy.

Gabe headed over to a corner piled with boxes. 'I'm going to set up some tables for people to make their own wreaths and decorations. Could you help me put together some samples?'

'Of course.'

He lifted a cardboard flap in one deft movement and looked at the contents. 'I thought these were wreaths.'

'What arc they?'

'Mistletoe balls.'

Etta couldn't help herself. Despite the knowledge that it was puerile she chuckled, and in response his expression morphed and his lips quirked up into a smile.

'Oh, Lord. I *am* sorry,' Etta said. 'I'm behaving like a schoolgirl. Please show me your mistletoe balls.'

With that his lips parted and he started to laugh,

and Etta joined in. A full-blown, belly-deep laugh that only eventually subsided.

'OK. Let's try again,' he said as he took various items out of the box, along with a set of instructions.

'I've done this before.' Etta pulled out a strand of wire and some string and handed it to him. 'You need to bend the wire into a circle and then twist the string round and round in loops until it's all covered. Then do the same again and join the two of them together to make a round shape. Twist the mistletoe around it, thread the berries and roses on and voila!'

'You make it sound easy.'

'It's a little fiddly, but it's a great idea for the fair. Kids *and* adults will enjoy it.'

As she twisted the wire she cast one more look around the room. 'For a man who doesn't like Christmas you've really surpassed yourself.'

'This is nothing to do with my feelings about Christmas. This is about making the event a success.' His tone of voice was firm as he bent his golden head to the task. 'This is a work project, aimed at maximising publicity and making money for the manor.'

'But it's not only about money—it's about the celebration of Christmas. I don't see how you can produce this and *not* have a tiny tendril of Christmas spirit buried somewhere.'

'Nope.' The sigh he puffed out was filled with exasperation. 'Why does it matter to you?'

It was a good question. 'Because I don't understand it. You have parents, siblings… Derwent Manor is an idyllic place to celebrate Christmas—you have everything I was desperate to give Cathy—and yet you say Christmas means nothing to you.'

Every Christmas she'd felt that surge of guilt, wished that Cathy had kind, loving grandparents, thought about the adoptive sister she'd barely known. Rosa… Small blonde Rosa—Etta's sister, Cathy's aunt.

'It doesn't feel fair.'

There was a silence, and then he picked up a piece of mistletoe, his movements deliberate. 'Things aren't always how they seem.'

Before he could elaborate his mobile phone shrilled out and he picked it up.

'Kaitlin.'

CHAPTER NINE

PHEW. RELIEF HIT him at the sound of his sister's voice. The last thing he wanted to do was swap Christmas memories with Etta. The obvious choice was to lie and back up the misleading articles the Derwent publicity machine rolled out every so often. Extol the supposed virtues of an aristocratic Christmas complete with family traditions and a sumptuous tree.

But he didn't want to fib to Etta—not when she clearly had a few Christmas demons of her own lurking...a fact betokened by the wistfulness, sadness and guilt that had skimmed over her expression. Yet the idea of sharing the details of Derwent Christmases didn't sit well with him—the awkwardness, the stilted conversations, the knowledge that his parents had little to say to their children other than homilies, the lack of joy or fun...

'Gabe?'

His sister's voice pulled him back to the present.

'You OK, Kaitlin?' It occurred to him how rare

it was for him to receive a call from his sister, especially in the past year.

'I'm fine.' Her voice was flat. 'I wondered if I could come back while the fair's on. Maybe help out?'

'That would be great. The only reason I didn't ask you is that Mum and Dad said you wouldn't be around because you had commitments with Frederick.'

Kaitlin's romance with Prince Frederick of Lycander was well-documented, and the tabloids were poised, waiting for an engagement announcement.

'Are you both coming?'

'Nope. Just me, if that's OK?'

Gabe frowned. There was an almost desperate undertone to Kaitlin's voice—a far cry from her usual serenity.

'Of course it is. This is your home and you can come here whenever you like. You don't need my permission or anyone else's.'

Though maybe that wasn't strictly true—he had little doubt that his parents were as avid as any reporter for news of an engagement, and would barricade Kaitlin from the manor until it came, if necessary. An alliance with royalty would have whetted the Derwents' ambition.

'Thanks, Gabe. I'll let you know my ETA.'

'OK. But I should warn you: April Fothering-ton will be here covering the fair.'

A sigh of resignation travelled over the miles. 'Please don't tell her in advance that I'll be there. I'll talk to her, but I'd rather do it off the cuff. I don't suppose you could announce *your* engagement, or create some sort of diversion? Something to take the heat off me?'

His frown deepened as worry kicked in—his sister usually revelled in the heat of the public's glare, shone in the spotlight with an even brighter glow than he did.

'Hold on, Kait. Is there something I should know?'

'Everything's fine.'

'You don't have to say that.'

'Yes, I do. I don't think *you're* fine—I don't even know where you've been the past nine months—but you won't tell me what's wrong, will you?'

'No.'

The laugh she gave was brittle. 'There you are, then. I'm fine. But you *can* give me some advice.'

'Shoot.'

'Do you think I should marry Prince Frederick?'

Talk about a loaded question... But Gabe sensed that if he didn't answer now Kaitlin would never ask again. 'He has a lot to offer. He's a prince, and he seems like a nice guy. You would have a more than comfortable life, and you were brought up to be a princess. You'd do an amazing job. Your children would be well off and privileged. You'd have fame and fortune and the opportunity to do some good.'

'In other words you think it would be a good alliance?'

'Yes.'

'Thank you, Gabe. I needed to hear that.'

Her voice had regained a level of serenity, yet he felt a qualm twinge.

'I'll see you soon.'

Gabe dropped his phone into his pocket and dismissed the doubt. His reasoning was spot-on—an alliance with Prince Frederick of Lycander would ensure Kaitlin's happiness.

A glance at Etta showed her with her head discreetly bent over the mistletoe decoration as she deftly threaded red beads into place. Brain whirring, he walked across the room, re-seated himself and picked up his own creation.

'Kaitlin is coming to the fair,' he said. 'I'd appreciate it if you don't mention your role in researching the new family tree to her.'

His sister knew as well as he did that his parents

had no interest in their ancestors, and he didn't want Etta's suspicions to be aroused. Especially now she had served her purpose.

Emotions seethed in his gut—emotions he had in lockdown even though the name of the man who might found a new Fairfax dynasty reverberated in his brain. Matteas John Coleridge.

Enough.

A small frown creased her brow and he could sense her curiosity.

'OK. I won't say a word.'

'Appreciated.'

'No problem.' Another bead was threaded, and with the air of breaching a conversational chasm Etta said, 'So, you never got round to telling me why you are so *Bah humbug* about Christmas.'

Reprieve over.

'I'm not *Bah humbug*. I'm just indifferent. Christmas hasn't ever been a big deal in our family. When I was a child I thought the best bit was the Church service in the morning—I loved the ritual of it…the words…the tradition. But after that it was always business as usual. The staff all used to have the day off, but Sarah always left us something to heat up.'

The awkwardness of those childhood Christmas lunches would live with him for ever.

'You must have enjoyed the presents? All children love to open their stockings.'

'My parents didn't do stockings. Their view was that presents should be functional, and we all understood that it was more important to put money back into the estate rather than accumulate useless clutter. They forbade us from giving them presents or giving each other gifts as well—they always said the best present we could give them was the forfeiture of our pocket money.'

Etta looked as though she were picking her words carefully. 'I get that the estate is important, but presents don't have to be expensive...'

'Inexpensive gifts came under the "useless clutter" umbrella, I guess.'

In all honesty the lack of presents hadn't been an issue. What he'd hated was the lack of any enjoyment. There had been no sitting down to watch a film or play board games, no laughter, nor much conversation, even. Though he knew he had little to complain about—he'd been fed, clothed, warm and safe.

'It's no big deal. There were times when we entertained over Christmas—that was much more festive.'

Although soon enough Gabe had understood that each occasion served a purpose, or forged an alliance, all with the idea of furthering the House of Derwent. So he and Kaitlin had learnt how to perform, how to charm and behave as befitted a Derwent, and that way he'd finally won his parents' approval—the holy grail that all three children had always craved.

'Tell me about *your* childhood Christmases.'

'There's not much to say. I was an only child for years, and Christmas was always quiet. I vowed that one day I'd have loads of kids—that I'd marry someone with an enormous family and Christmas would be packed with frivolity and fun and festivities.'

The look on her face was wistful, as if she could see that dream Christmas before her.

'That didn't pan out, but Cathy and I always have a fab day. We get up at dawn and open our stockings—lots of fun gifts, like mugs, chocolates, jewellery… Then we have a pancake breakfast and a long walk before we cook Christmas dinner with Christmas music turned up high. We eat, open more presents, watch films, play games, eat chocolate… It's a great day. I do my best to make up for the lack of family.'

He threaded another bead onto the wire ring and eyed her. Curiosity percolated through him as to why she'd given up on her dream. 'It's not too late for you to marry and have more kids. Not because you want a suitable dad for Cathy, but because it's what *you* want.'

'I told you—marriage is not for me. As for more kids... I have considered adoption, but I know what a big step that is to take.'

It was a step he would never take; because it wouldn't be fair. The law stated that an adopted child could not inherit his title. So no way could he adopt a son and bring him up on an estate he could never inherit. And somehow to adopt a girl just because her gender meant she couldn't inherit seemed wrong.

For a second, desolation touched him, but he pushed it away, focused instead on Etta. There was no reason why she couldn't have the future she'd once envisaged. 'Perhaps it's the right step for you? But what about the other part of that dream? The husband and the in-laws and the whole big family Christmas?'

'It's not going to happen. I think I'm missing the necessary gene.'

Her voice was light but it masked sadness, and now the air felt awhirl with dreams that had bitten the dust. Both his and hers. Dreams of families seated around dining tables, children opening presents under the Christmas tree… His dreams couldn't be resurrected, but maybe hers could.

'Rubbish.'

'No, it's not! I told you. I've tried dating and it…it doesn't work out.'

'And I told *you* you're dating the wrong men.' He surveyed her. 'I bet you're going for nice, average men with nice, respectable jobs and—'

'What's wrong with that?' Colour climbed her cheekbones and she narrowed her eyes.

'Physical attraction is important too.'

'I don't see why that can't grow with time.'

Gabe raised his eyebrows. 'For *real*? Has that worked for you so far? *Sheesh!* You told me you've ended up dancing at your dates' weddings to other women. Not the best track record.'

'So what do you suggest?'

'That you date someone you feel attracted to in a physical way—where there's a spark.'

'Maybe that gene is missing too.'

'I don't believe that.'

The last berry slipped onto the ring and he stood and held up the mistletoe circle, attached it to the waiting ring.

'Look up.'

A hesitation and then she did as he asked, her

face tipped up towards him, her delicate angled features bathed in the flicker of light.

'Kiss me and I'll show you,' he said. 'The ball's in your court. Literally.'

His throat constricted, his breath massed in his lungs, and then slowly Etta rose to her feet and stepped forward until she was flush against him. Hesitantly her hands came up and looped around his neck. Her fingers touched his nape and desire shuddered through his body. And then she stood on tiptoe and touched her lips against his in sweet hesitation.

Her lips parted in a sigh of pleasure and he deepened the kiss. For a heartbeat she hesitated, and then her body relaxed, melted against his, and he pulled her closer, inhaled her vanilla scent, tasted a tang of peppermint. Then sweetness morphed into more—into a fierce intensity of sheer sensation as need grew.

Until she pulled away and stood with eyes wide as their ragged breaths mingled.

'I...'

Panic filled the tawny brown eyes and her lips twisted into a line that spelled mortification.

Gabe tried to pull his frazzled brain cells together—knew he had to stop her before she ran.

'It's OK, Etta.'

'No. It isn't. That was unprofessional and wrong...'

'It wasn't. It was a kiss. Between two consenting adults who are attracted to each other. It wasn't wrong. It was a kiss to show you that you aren't missing a gene.'

Etta shook her head, swiped her hand across her mouth. 'I want to forget this ever happened.'

The day of the fair dawned cold and crisp. Etta woke up and assessed the weather with relief. The sky was clear—a bright blue studded with the cotton wisp of a few clouds. It would be cold, but there would be no need to move everything inside.

Swinging her legs out of bed, she let her brain list her extensive to-do list.

On the list was meeting Kaitlin Derwent. Gabe's sister would fly in early the next day. Curiosity resurfaced as to why Gabe wanted to keep the new family tree secret from his sister. Surely that took the idea of a surprise present a step too far? Not that Etta would ask him—she had gone out of her way to avoid any non-work-related conversation with him since The Kiss.

Mortification still roiled through her tummy at the memory—how *could* she have kissed him like that? A sheer cascade of desire had overwhelmed

every iota of sense and she had given in, lost perspective and thrown self-respect aside. *Stupid.*
And worse was the fact that for Gabe it had been
nothing more than an object lesson, to show her
that she could feel passion. Well, Etta didn't *want*
to feel passion—or at least not on that scale. It was
too much, too dizzying, too everything.

Thank goodness that in two days she'd be out
of here—away from Gabe and his ability to un-
settle her. Instead she'd be on board a cruise ship,
reunited with Cathy.

Excitement fizzed inside her, but like it or not it
was underlain with a soupçon of sadness. A sadness she *always* felt at the end of a project. The
second she saw her daughter again all thoughts
of Derwent Manor, family trees and *especially*
Gabe Derwent would flee her brain. She knew
it. It had to be like that. She couldn't let passion
overcome family bonds ever again. Especially
now. Because once the euphoria of seeing Cathy
faded she needed to explain the relocation plan
to her daughter.

Fifteen minutes later there was the familiar
knock on the door that heralded Gabe.

'Morning. You all set for the day?'

As ever, no sign of tension was on display, and
not for the first time she envied his ability to surf

over all circumstances with unshakable confidence. The same confidence that meant he appeared to have had no problem whitewashing The Kiss from his memory banks. Not that it had been a capital letter event in his opinion—and that thought intensified her humiliation a hundred fold.

'Ready and looking forward to it.'

A few hours later and the fair was in full swing; Etta gazed round at the incredible display on offer. It was easy to believe that she'd stepped back in time.

Inside the manor, the staff were kitted out as Victorian servants. Parlour maids in simple black dresses, chambermaids in print dresses, both complete with frilled apron and cap, bustled about, engaged in their household tasks, and they were all able to discuss the duties expected of servants in the Victorian era.

Sarah reigned supreme in the hustle and bustle of the kitchen, in the throes of the preparation of a lavish Christmas dinner. The scents were evocative of Christmas—cranberries bubbling over the fire, the aroma of chestnut, sugar and candied fruit mingling with the savoury scent of roast turkey and freshwater smelt. Families watched and asked eager questions.

Etta glanced round and saw the lengthening queue for Christmas punch. It looked as if they needed some help.

As she approached the table Eileen, a teenage girl from the village school who'd volunteered her services, smiled in relief. 'It's manic! I'm not allowed to handle the rum, and my mum came over all faint, and…and…'

'You're doing a grand job. Hand over a spare pinny and a hat and I'll get mixing.'

Soon enough the good-natured jostle of the queue became manageable, with everyone happy to hand over the cost for a plastic cup of Roman Punch—a judicious mix of rum and lemon and near frozen dissolved sugar.

'I'd better move on,' Etta said as she saw Gabe gesturing to her to follow him.

'Thank you for that,' he said as they exited the kitchen.

He smiled down at her and the world seemed to shrink. The sounds of the fair faded and his smile warmed her, curled her toes, and that wretched kiss sprang to the forefront of her mind. His eyes darkened, the same way they had when they'd locked lips, and a stupid feeling of gratification streamed through her veins at the knowledge that just maybe he *did* remember those magical moments.

Hold it together. Even if Gabe had been affected it would *not* be a smart move to grab the man and have a replay.

'No problem. It's the least I can do.'

As they stepped outside into the crisp air she gestured around.

'You must be thrilled—the place is packed and people are having an amazing time.'

The outside area buzzed with noise and laughter overlaid with the exquisite sound of the local choir, whose pure voices filled the air with Christmas carols. Children raced around a designated part of the lawn with hoops and sticks, and in another part a boisterous game of quoits was underway. The smell of roasting chestnuts tantalised her tastebuds, and everywhere Victorian re-enactors roamed chatting to the visitors.

'It's a true extravaganza! A day everyone will remember.'

There was that smile again, and she would swear her hair had frizzed. Time for a breather.

'I'll go check out the stalls. I want to find extra gifts for Cathy and Martha and Steph.'

He frowned.

'I'll be fine, Gabe. In two days' time I'll have to fend for myself.'

The words were a timely reminder as she headed off.

Authentic-looking Victorian toys glinted in the light of the December sun, and delight filled her as she browsed the beautifully crafted spinning tops and Victorian dolls. Her gaze landed on a stunning jewellery box that Steph would adore. As she ran her finger over the glossy wood, with its inlay of mother-of-pearl and gold leaf, she could picture her friend's appreciation of the two-tier box.

But before she could ask the price her neck prickled and she spun round.

'Hello, Etta.'

Tommy stood there, dark hair slicked back, a leather jacket over a white T-shirt, a swagger in his stance.

'Fancy seeing you here. I knew I'd get you alone if I was patient. I've been watching you.'

His voice was low—friendly, even—but Etta recognised the underlying menace. Tommy was at his cruellest when he sounded his most pleasant, and a cold drop of fear ran down her spine.

'Hardly alone,' she reminded him, her hand darting to the panic button round her neck. *No.*

She would not cause a scene—would not cast a shadow over the success of the fair.

'But minus Sir Toff. I wanted another chat.'

'I have nothing to say to you.'

'But I want to talk to you. In person. I *like* the personal touch, Etta. You know that. You remember my personal touch, don't you?'

Now fear burned cold and she stepped back, unable to help the instinctive movement. 'This is getting old, Tommy. Please leave.' Brave words, given that her insides were roiling.

'But this is a new message—a Christmas greeting. I've decided that this Christmas should be a nice family affair—you and me and our daughter, sitting down to a nice roast dinner, cooked the way I like it.'

'You've lost the plot, because that is *not* happening. You're not family.'

'I think Cathy might disagree. That's why you've hidden her away isn't it? But I know you'll be spending Christmas with her.' Then his expression altered. 'Ah, here comes Mr Toff now.'

Relief doused her in a wave as Gabe arrived, the warmth of his muscular body next to her shielding her. 'Get off my land. Now.'

'It's a public event, Toff. My money is as good

as anyone's. And I'm sure you don't want to cause
a scene.'

'I have no problem with a scene. You're leaving now. Either of your own volition or with my
assistance...'

Malevolence lit Tommy's eyes and Etta tensed,
braced herself in that old familiar response.

His dark eyes rested on her for a second and
then he stepped back, his hands in the air. 'Nice
try. But I don't brawl any more. I'm a nice, peace-
able man who has seen the error of my ways. All
I want is the chance to be a father.'

He winked at Etta and bile rose in her throat.

'I'll be on my way...but I'll be seeing you.
Happy Christmas!'

With that he vanished into the crowd.

The whole confrontation had taken no more
than a few moments, but those minutes had left
her encased in a mesh of terror.

Gabe was on his phone, giving a description of
Tommy and asking for confirmation that he'd left
the grounds.

He dropped his phone into his pocket. 'You
OK?'

'I'm fine.' Aware that a few spectators were
nudging each other, Etta forced a smile to her

face. 'Absolutely fine. Isn't it time to judge the Victorian Christmas reindeer?'

Gabe hesitated.

'It's OK, Gabe. This is my problem now. Our deal is nearly done.'

CHAPTER TEN

GABE EXHALED HEAVILY. His muscles ached, but the clear-down was finally finished, with everything set in place for a rerun the following day.

'Thank you, everyone. The day was an outstanding success. You have my heartfelt thanks and I've put my wallet behind the bar in the pub. Drinks on me tonight. Go and enjoy.'

There was a cheer and the staff filed out, leaving just Etta and himself in the enormous marquee that held the restaurant. Exhaustion smudged her features and dust smeared the jeans she had changed into for the clear-down. She'd worked like the proverbial trooper—she'd served food, played games, and done more than her share of lugging crates and boxes. But he was pretty sure her pallor had *zip* to do with work and everything to do with Tommy.

'Come on. We definitely deserve a drink.'

Now her lips turned up in a smile and his breath caught at her sheer prettiness; there was an ageless quality to her beauty—the kind that came from character and poise.

His palms itched with a desire to swirl her into his arms and kiss her, take her mind off Tommy. *Bad idea, Gabe. Been there, done that.* And whilst their kiss had blown his mind, it had spooked Etta—she'd been clear that she wanted to forget it. He didn't get why, but instinct told him the reasons were complicated. If Etta wanted to act on their mutual attraction it had to be her decision, not his.

'A drink sounds good—and I have just the thing,' she said.

He followed her to the kitchen, where she headed to the fridge.

'I know it's probably not as high-quality as you're used to, but I picked us up a bottle of bubbles. To toast the success of the fair.'

The unexpectedness of the gesture halted him in his tracks.

'Don't look so surprised.'

'I *am* surprised. The Derwents don't go in for celebratory gestures because success is a given. Thank you.'

'You're very welcome. That must be hard,' she added. 'To always expect to succeed.'

'I've never really thought about it.'

'Hmm. Well, I don't always succeed, and I'm not sure how successful our dinner is going to be either. I told Sarah she didn't need to cook for us today—she needs to go home and put her feet up, ready for tomorrow. So I made something yesterday! Don't get your hopes up—it's not exactly haute cuisine. Just macaroni cheese and salad, but...'

'Etta, stop apologising. This is a lovely gesture.'

And in truth he didn't know how to handle it.

She pulled the macaroni cheese out of the fridge and put it into the oven, while he opened the sparkling wine, the pop of the cork reverberating round the room. He poured the frothing golden liquid into two crystal flutes and handed one over.

'Cheers.'

'Cheers. To a successful alliance. Your new family tree is done, the fair is on its way to success, and after tomorrow I'll be out of your hair.'

There was a hint of strain to her smile, and he put his glass down on the counter.

'You must be looking forward to seeing Cathy again. I'll drop you at the airport as planned.'

Etta was flying out to New York to meet up with the cruise ship.

'Actually, there's no need.'

He raised his eyebrows. 'It's no bother—it's all

part of the contract, and I want to make sure you get on board safe. Especially now Tommy has turned up. Again.'

'No. I mean there's no need because I'm not going. I've decided to stay home. Tommy made it clear that he intends to gatecrash Christmas, and I can't risk leading him to Cathy.'

'You can't let Tommy dictate your actions. Even if he did make it to the cruise ship, Security would deal with him. Hell. I'll speak to the captain.'

Etta shook her head, her chin tilted outward. 'Thank you, Gabe, but I'm still staying put.'

'Then Tommy wins.'

'No, *I* win. Because I know Cathy is safe.'

'So what happens after Christmas? Are you *never* going to see Cathy again?' He knew he shouldn't sound so angry but frustration clenched his jaw, caused him to pace the tiled kitchen floor.

'Of course not. I'll work out a way for us to meet up and then we'll take off for a while.'

'What about her education?'

'It will be like an early gap year. She will be experiencing life.'

'What about money?'

'I've still got some savings left, and I'll let my London flat out... I'll waitress. I'll manage. It won't be for long—I *know* Tommy will end up behind bars again.'

'You cannot let Tommy screw your life up. At least give Cathy a shot at meeting him and recognising him for the creep he is.'

Her face flushed and her hands clenched into fists. 'You don't understand, Gabe. You can't.'

'Try me.'

'I will *not* let Cathy's life be tainted or flawed by that man. He's evil. He…' Her voice caught, and her brown eyes were dark with a maelstrom of memories. 'He is capable of charm—he weaves a spell that sucks you in. He will pull Cathy in.'

'You don't *know* that.' Why was she so stubborn about this?

'No, I don't. But no way will I risk it.' The laugh she gave was mirthless. 'Think about it like an investment strategy. This is a commodity I will keep safe at any cost. I know Tommy. He entices you in but once he's enmeshed you it all changes. He hurt me, Gabe, and worse than that he made me believe I deserved it. That I was nothing.'

The anger that swept over him shocked him with its extremity. If Tommy were here right now he would crush him. Yet he sensed there was something more at stake here than Etta's fear that Cathy would be sucked in.

'I understood why you ran from him when you were a teenager. I don't understand why you would run now. Not without giving Cathy a shot at seeing what a loser Tommy is.'

'I can't. I won't take the risk.'

Her voice was flat. Gabe studied her closed expression and realisation struck. Etta was terrified that she would lose Cathy—believed that Cathy would forsake her at the drop of a hat.

'I've made my mind up, Gabe, and I won't discuss it further. Please—can we drink fizz, eat macaroni cheese, and think about the fair tomorrow?'

The tiredness in her voice swayed him into acquiescence—that, alongside the knowledge that it was her decision to make. Their deal was nearly over and he had other fish to fry. A twist of his gut was a reminder of his own Christmas plans and what he needed to be focused on—the future of the Dukedom of Fairfax was at stake.

'Fizz and macaroni cheese it is.'

Distraction therapy at its best.

The second day of the fair dawned even brighter, and Etta was determined to enjoy the day and keep all thoughts of her lonely Christmas to come at bay.

As she entered the kitchen she paused in the doorway at the sight of Kaitlin Derwent, seated at the table.

Every bit as stunning in the flesh as her photographs indicated, Kaitlin was dressed in a gorgeous hand-embroidered dress that brought out the Titian shade of her hair and showed off a figure that combined svelteness with curves. But before Etta could even register envy Kaitlin rose and smiled a poster-girl smile that she couldn't help but return.

'You must be Etta. Gabe told me how much help you've been with the fair.'

Etta glanced across at Gabe, who was standing at the counter pouring cereal into a bowl, and her heart gave its familiar annoying hop, skip, and jump. This would be the last time she witnessed the Earl of Wycliffe at breakfast, and she allowed herself a sneaky glance at the breadth of his torso, the strength of his features, the spike of his blond hair. A glimmer of regret struck her—the first man in years her body was interested in and she'd passed up the opportunity to follow it up.

Ridiculous. No regret necessary. She'd made a mature decision not to succumb to an over-the-top attraction.

The Kiss flashed into her mind. *See—an exact*

case in point. The Kiss had been a humdinger and very much over the top.

Turning resolutely back to Kaitlin, she smiled. 'I've had a great time.'

'I need to freshen up and then I'll be ready for duty.'

'We'll catch up properly later,' Gabe said with a small crease on his brow as he watched his sister leave the room. He turned to Etta. 'I need you to stick with Kaitlin today.'

'She may not want me to do that.'

'Tough. I want to keep an eye on both of you, and that will be easier if you're together.'

'Fine.'

She could only hope Kaitlin wouldn't mind. After all, Lady Kaitlin Derwent was used to a social circle way more sophisticated than Etta's.

As it turned out, Kaitlin seemed more than happy to hang out with her, and Etta could only stand back in admiration as the red-haired woman walked around the fair, exuding charm.

'Come on,' Kaitlin said eventually. 'I'll buy you a drink.'

Minutes later they were seated at the back of the marquee.

'So, how have you got along with Gabe?' Kaitlin asked.

'Fine.'

The redhead hesitated. 'Are the two of you an item?'

'No. Absolutely not. No. *Ick.*'

Ick? Where had *that* come from? Etta took a gulp of punch, welcoming the hit of rum as Kaitlin's perfectly arched eyebrows rose.

'Hey, Gabe's not that bad. Most women would bite your arm off for the opportunity to spend time with him.'

'I'm not "most women".'

'Well, he's not most men. I know Lady Isobel didn't do him any favours, but Gabe is a good man. Bet he hasn't told you about his charity work.'

'What charity work?'

But before Kaitlin could answer she looked across the tent and muttered a most unladylike curse. 'What's wrong?' Etta asked.

'April Fotherington is headed this way.' Kaitlin stood up. 'I'd rather face her outside.'

Once they were on the lawn Etta saw the dark-haired reporter sashaying towards them with a predatory gleam in her eye.

If Kaitlin was nervous it was impossible to see; her lips were upturned in a smile of welcome with a hint of coolness. 'April. Lovely to see you.'

'And such a surprise. My sources had you at a function in Lycander, with Prince Frederick and the rest of the Lycander Royals.'

'It was a last-minute decision.'

'Hmm… I hope all is well with you and the Prince? I did hear a little rumour that the Lycanders had been hoping for a match with a Princess.'

'I'd like to think that the Prince will make up his own mind about his marriage.'

Kaitlin's voice was even, but Etta could sense the tension that vibrated from her body.

Before April could answer Gabe arrived, his body seemingly relaxed as he stood next to his sister in definitive alliance.

'So no rift?' April persevered.

'None.'

Kaitlin's composure was enviable—due, no doubt, to a lifetime in the public eye.

'Hmm…' The reporter's tone hinted at scepticism. 'I'm glad to hear it. So, what about your Christmas plans? Will you be jetting back to Lycander for the Christmas Eve celebrations? They are spectacular. I was there last year, covering a story on the Prince and Sunita Greenberg—the model he was supposedly serious about. Before *you* came on the scene, of course.'

'Of course.'

Again her voice was level, but now a slightly strained quality had entered Kaitlin's smile and Etta could sense the effort it took for her to hold her body poised.

Gabe stepped forward. 'Easy does it, April. You're here to cover the fair—not grill my sister on her personal life.' There was a steely undertone to his voice.

'Good point.' April turned her green gaze, alight with calculation, to Etta.

Great. Unfortunately she *didn't* have a lifetime of experience in the public eye, and a feeling of foreboding prickled her skin.

'I *do* have a question about the fair. Etta, you have done a fabulous job—the Victorian theme is spot-on...accurate to the last detail...'

The 'but' loomed, travelling at warp speed, and Etta braced herself.

'But I am a little confused. You've been here for over three weeks. It seems a little over the top for a consultant role. Makes me wonder if there's something else going on here... Any other aspect to your role...'

Keep calm. This was a fishing expedition—April couldn't know about her work on the new family tree and was way more likely to be angling for a romance story.

Etta opened her mouth, summoned the evasion. 'Well…fairs like this need a lot of planning.'

'I understand that. But your role wasn't to plan the whole event, but simply to consult over historical accuracy. I'm not sure I understand why that necessitated such a long stay here. I was wondering if maybe you were hired for something else. Maybe you're writing a book, Gabe? Or maybe…'

Etta's mind raced. Any minute now April would mention the possibility of her researching a new family tree and she knew her face would give away the truth.

Then Gabe stepped forward and took her hand in his, gave it a squeeze that conveyed warning. 'OK, April. We're busted.'

Say what? They were?

Apprehension sliced at her tummy even as she did her best to keep her expression neutral. No need to panic. Clearly Gabe was in possession of a plan.

'I did hire Etta to help with the fair, but once she'd been here a few days…well, we got to know each other better and what we saw we liked so…'

'So the two of you are an item?' April's gaze skittered from Gabe to Etta and back again, suspicion mingling with the hope of a nice juicy story.

Etta remained stock still, her head awhirl with

disbelief. Gabe wasn't in possession of a plan—
the man was clearly possessed.

Suspicion won out and April shook her head.
'And you've just stayed buried in the countryside
for weeks? I haven't heard even a whisper of gossip. No fancy dinners? No parties?'

'The fair took precedence. But I'm going to
make it up to Etta. We're off on a Christmas break
to Vienna. Surprise, sweetheart!'

Ah! Surprise was an emotion she could do!
Right now she could be more surprised than anyone. 'Vienna…?' she whispered.

Sweetheart?

'Yup. What do you think?'

She thought she wanted to clock him on the
head, pull on her trainers and leg it over the horizon. An alternative would be to identify this fabri-
cation as being exactly that… But Gabe wouldn't
do this without good reason. Right?

'Um…I sure am surprised,' she managed.

April's gaze was focused on her. 'You obviously
weren't expecting this? You must be thrilled to be
Lady Isobel's successor.'

Fantastic. This gets better and better.

Good reason or not, she would not go along
with this.

But before she could open her mouth Gabe kept right on.

'Lady Isobel is the past—it's the present I'm most interested in, and I'm looking forward to Christmas with Etta. But right now we need to get on with our fair duties.' He turned away and then back. 'Oh, incidentally, I believe that this also explains Kaitlin's sudden arrival on the scene. Am I right, sis?'

Kaitlin didn't so much as blink a perfectly made-up eyelid. 'Busted too!'

An expressive lift of her elegant shoulders and a full-wattage authentic Kaitlin Derwent smile accompanied the words. AKA the barefaced lie.

'I spoke to Gabe and curiosity got to me. I wanted to meet Etta in person.'

Etta gave up, pasted a smile on her face and watched the Derwents in action. Waited until the reporter finally left to cover the fair and then spun round to face Gabe. 'What the—?'

'Not now. People are watching, and April isn't a fool. I'll explain later.'

Etta was pretty damn sure that steam must be rising from her in visible waves. 'No, you won't. You will explain right now,' she hissed. 'We can go into the private bit of the house. I'm sure everyone will understand that we need some privacy, given our "relationship".'

Kaitlin glanced from one to another. 'I think Etta has a point. I can hold the fort at the fair. You clearly need some quality time alone together.'

CHAPTER ELEVEN

GABE WOULDN'T EXACTLY call this 'quality time'. He watched as Etta strode up and down the already threadbare carpet, practically sparking with anger.

'What the *hell* did you think you were doing? Because there is no way in this universe or any other, parallel or perpendicular, that we are going to Vienna.'

No preamble, then.

'I was salvaging the situation. A minute later and April would have rumbled the family tree surprise for my father.'

'So? Who cares? I get it you want it to be a surprise, but this is a bit extreme, don't you think?'

'Look, I understand you're angry.'

'Angry? I'm *livid*. I'm a *thesaurus* of angry.'

Each furious pace showed that.

'But it's done. At the time it seemed like the best solution. It helped Kaitlin out and…'

And it meant he could keep his role of bodyguard, make sure Etta remained safe from Tommy whilst she perfected her relocation plan.

'Now the whole world thinks we're an item. Exactly what I *didn't* want.'

'I know, and I apologise for that, but I had hoped Christmas in Vienna would make up for it.'

Etta screeched to a halt. 'Why would you think that?'

'Because it will beat spending Christmas by yourself, missing Cathy and hiding from Tommy.'

Etta narrowed her eyes. 'I didn't even know you were going to Vienna.'

Neither had he until a few days ago, when he'd discovered that Matteas Coleridge lived in Vienna and played the cello in a renowned Viennese orchestra. The knowledge had triggered a visceral need to see the man who might one day step into his shoes. Just see him—Gabe had no intent of making contact. Not yet. But he wanted to see him in his own environment.

'It seemed like a good idea. Rather than rattling around here on my own.'

'Why take *me*? What's in it for you? I can understand why you'd take a real girlfriend, but why me?'

Because taking a girlfriend would effectively take the spotlight well and truly away from his real motivation. He had a lot of respect for April's tenacity and instinct for a story. If she got wind of the new family tree there was a chance she'd pull the real story together.

There was also a chance Etta would do the same—hence his first choice of girlfriend *wouldn't* have been Etta. But he'd had to move fast and he had decided to take the risk. Yes, she knew Matteas Coleridge's name, but there must be lots of Matt Coleridges in the world, and with any luck she wouldn't even realise that it was the name of a member of a twenty-piece orchestra. If she did, he'd deal with it.

'I have my reasons.'

'Now is *not* the time to be a man of mystery. I'm sure you do have your reasons—I want to know what they are.'

'No.'

Hands slammed onto her hips. 'No?'

'No. This is the deal on offer. You let April run with this romance story until after the New Year. You come to Vienna with me. In return I extend your contract and pay you an additional fee. I'll throw in the bodyguard service as well. An added bonus is that you'll lead Tommy far away from Cathy. That's the deal. If you don't like it, don't accept it. Feel free to call April. Tell her it's off, that you've changed your mind. Tell her the truth—tell her I made it up.'

'If I do that what would you do?'

'Find another girlfriend and take her to Vienna.'

Even if the idea didn't sit well with him, given his reason for going to Vienna it would be simpler to have a fake girlfriend rather than a real one.

'So the ball's back in your court.'

The following day Etta gazed around at the interior of the private jet. En route to Vienna. Disbelief sat alongside her consideration as to whether or not she had lost her mind.

How had Gabe manoeuvred her into a position where she had actually *agreed* to this harebrained scheme? Well, firstly there had been the sheer impossibility of any explanation to April. How to clarify why she'd gone along with it all, posed for photos, agreed to everything? Plus the idea had filled her with discomfort—it reeked of snitching, and it would drop both Gabe and Kaitlin in it. Mind you, she had little doubt that Gabe would pull himself out, no problem, but still...

Then there had been the internal debate: Christmas in Vienna, versus Christmas holed up in her flat or at an anonymous motel? True, Vienna came with the price tag of Gabe, but if she didn't go he'd

take someone else. And she loathed the concept—
her fingers had curled into fists at the thought.
Not from jealousy. But from anticipated mortification. Everyone would think she'd been passed
over for a newer model.

In addition, the element of curiosity had popped
right up—every historian's instinct inside her told
her there was something off about all this. *Why*
did Gabe want to go to Vienna? *Why* didn't he
want anyone to know about the new family tree?

And lastly her treacherous body had seen some
definite potential benefits. Benefits endorsed by
her conversation with Steph.

Her best friend had been thrilled for her. 'Go for
it,' she'd instructed. 'For once in your life, Etta,
let your hair down, put on your dancing shoes,
and do the Viennese waltz. Quit worrying and
go with the flow.'

Cathy had advised much the same. 'Mum, I am
so happy for you. Now we can all enjoy Christmas because we know you won't be alone. Enjoy
yourself—and don't worry.'

Easier said than done. Worry was paramount as
she gazed round the luxurious interior—somehow
the idea of a spacious airborne room, complete
with sumptuous leather sofa, a boardroom table,

reclining seats and a screen that might grace any home cinema, represented the utterly over-the-top level of her own emotions.

No, not her emotions. This was all about her physical reactions—the rapid rate of her heart and the acceleration of her pulse as she gazed at him now, completely at his ease, his blue-grey eyes on her as she curled her legs beneath her in a false posture of relaxation.

His mobile rang and he glanced at the screen. 'Sorry, I need to take it.' Phone to his ear, he said, 'Cora, thanks for the callback. You need to call Kaitlin. I reckon she could do with some twin input—she actually asked for *my* advice.'

A pause.

'Yes, that's exactly what I told her. To consider it an alliance, a merger.'

A longer pause, and Etta couldn't help but hear the agitated squawk that emerged from Cora's end.

Then Gabe shrugged. 'I told it how I saw it. Kaitlin is cut out to be a princess. But I figure I'm not the authority on marriage—you're the one who has walked that walk to the altar.'

More talk and then he raised a hand in a gesture of affectionate exasperation.

'Spare me the lecture on love. Talk to Kaitlin.'

He disconnected with a shake of his head and Etta couldn't help but grin.

'You're close to your sisters.'

The observation sent a thread of sadness through her veins as a sudden image of Rosa strobed through her brain. The adoptive sister she hadn't seen for seventeen years.

Gabe shook his head. 'Not really. They were only two when I went to boarding school, so we never got close. And now we're adults we have pretty much gone our separate ways.'

'Why don't you do something about that? You're lucky to have siblings. Plus it's clear they care about you.'

His blue eyes held hers with an arrested look that bordered on startled. 'It is…?'

'Yes—it *is*. I don't mean to pry, but it sounds like Kaitlin isn't OK and that she came home to see you and ask your advice. And you *do* care about her—one of the reasons you stepped in with April was to help Kaitlin.'

'*One* of the reasons.' Gabe's voice was hard. 'Don't read something that isn't there. I stepped in with April to protect my own interests. Helping Kaitlin was a bonus.'

Why was he so resistant to the idea that he was

close to his sisters? 'So you wouldn't have helped her if it hadn't benefited you too?'

'I didn't say that. I'm just telling it as it is. We aren't a close, touchy-feely family.'

'You say that like it would be a bad thing if you were. I don't get that at all.'

Because *she* would love to somehow turn the clock back and be part of Rosa's life, and it made her mad that Gabe was bypassing something so important. The man was lucky enough to have family on tap and he didn't seem to care.

'It works for me.' Gabe looked at her, his eyes still angry. 'You said you were an only child "for years". So presumably you now have a sibling?'

For a moment she was tempted to deny it. *Not acceptable*. Bad enough that she wasn't part of her sister's life—to deny her existence would be wrong. Even if her parents *didn't* count her as being Rosa's sister. After all she didn't share the same bloodline—hadn't been in Rosa's life since Rosa was three.

'Yes. A sister. We've lost touch.'

'Then why not get *back* in touch?'

'It's complicated.'

And now she was regretting the whole conversation—Gabe's relationship with his sisters was none of her business. But now she'd made it her business and she'd opened up a conversational bear pit.

'Complicated how?'

'It doesn't matter.'

'Yes, it does. You've given *me* a hard time about my lack of brotherly support and now it turns out you've lost touch with your sister.'

Hmm… It seemed she'd touched a nerve, but Gabe had a point. What to do now?

Etta squared her shoulders—she would give him the facts. Or at least some of them.

'My parents gave me an ultimatum when I was pregnant. Them or the baby. I couldn't give my baby up and I haven't seen them since. Rosa was three at the time.'

The scene was still etched on her memory banks, however many times she'd tried to erase it.

Rosa in her mother's arms, the three-year-old's chubby legs wrapped round her mum's waist. The daughter her parents had always craved—blood of their blood. Her dad standing behind them. A tableau of the perfect family; no need nor space for Etta.

Her adoptive mother's voice. 'You can come back, Etta, and we'll do our duty by you. But not the baby. Give it up for adoption.'

'I can't do that.' The taste of tears as they rolled

down her cheeks, her hands outstretched in plea. 'I know I've done wrong, messed up big-time with Tommy, but I can't do that.'

There had been no relenting on her parents' faces.

'You have to. That baby has Tommy's genes— how can you want to keep it?'

Black knowledge had dawned—a dark understanding of why her parents had been unable to love her—they had always seen her as tainted by her unknown genes.

'I want to keep this baby because I already love him or her, and I don't care whose genes she has. Please try to understand. This is your grandchild. A part of me.'

She'd waited, but her parents had just stood there, lips pressed together. Rosa had looked on, knowing something was wrong, her lower lip wobbling. So Etta had taken a deep breath, stepped forward and dropped a kiss on Rosa's head, felt the little girl's blond curls tickling her nose.

'Goodbye, sweetheart.'

With that she'd left, one hand protectively cradling her tummy even as panic washed over her. All the time hoping, praying that they would call her back. But they hadn't.

Etta blinked, emerged from the vivid clarity of

the past and saw that Gabe was hunkered down in front of her chair. She realised a tear had escaped her eye and trickled a salty trail down her cheek.

He reached out and caught it on the tip of his thumb. 'I'm sorry, Etta. I can't imagine how that must have felt but I'm pretty sure it sucked.'

The temptation to throw herself on the breadth of his chest, inhale his scent, take reassurance and safety and comfort nigh on overwhelmed her.

Pull yourself together. She'd come to terms with her past long ago.

'No need for you to be sorry. It is what it is and I've come to terms with it. I'll never regret the choice I made.'

The idea of giving Cathy up had been an impossibility—her own birth parents had abandoned her, and maybe they'd had reason to, but she would not—could not—do that to her child.

'But I do regret that Cathy has no grandparents. And I regret Rosa not being part of her life. That's why I get mad when I see sibling relationships going to waste.'

He remained in front of her. His hand covered hers and awareness sparked.

'So Rosa must be nineteen…twenty now?'

'Yes. I send my parents a Christmas card every

year. In case they ever want to meet their grand-daughter.'

'Maybe you need to try and get in touch with Rosa directly. Could be your parents haven't told her about you *or* the Christmas cards.'

'That wouldn't be fair to anyone. Gabe, you don't need to come up with a strategy. My parents and I—we made our choices and we need to live with them.'

'Rosa didn't make a choice. I'm not advocating a reunion with your parents—I think what they did was wrong—but Rosa is different. She should be given a choice.'

'I won't be responsible for causing complications in Rosa's life. Or my parents'. That's my choice. Just like it's yours whether or not you build a closer relationship with Kaitlin and Cora. My point is that I envy you the opportunity to do so. I think you should build on what you have with Kaitlin and Cora.'

'Cora doesn't need me—she is incredibly happy.'

'Closeness isn't just about being there when someone needs you. You don't always have to be Mr Fix It.' Though now she came to think of it, that was what Gabe was—always looking for a solution, the optimum strategy.

'Right now there's nothing to fix. Cora's marriage seems to be working out.'

'Even though she has made a technically unsuitable alliance? With someone out of your social circle?'

'Actually, no. She has married someone with immense wealth—that's an asset. And it turns out Rafael also has connections with the elite of Spanish aristocracy, though the jury is out on whether *that* is a useful commodity or not.'

'But that isn't why Cora married him. She married him because she loves him. You can see how much they love each other.' She'd seen it at the Cavershams' Advent Ball—it was the same connection Ruby and Ethan had.

Gabe shrugged. 'His money will endure and grow. Rafael Martinez is a billionaire, with an incredibly astute grasp of business opportunities. His connections are handy. I assume Cora thinks love is a bonus.'

'No! You're missing the point. Cora probably thinks the *money and connections* are a bonus. She loves him regardless of those and she would have married him if he were penniless.'

'He wouldn't be Rafael Martinez if he were penniless.' He shrugged. 'I see what you're saying,

Etta, but I think they'd have been wiser to leave love out of the equation.'

'So you believe they're kidding themselves? That in reality they have married each other for money and titles and connection but they won't admit it?'

Why was he so anti-love? So sure every relationship was based on barter or an exchange of assets?

'Yes. And I think one or both of them will be hurt when the bubble bursts.'

'And you think it will be Cora?'

'Yes.'

'So what are you going to do about it?'

'Ram Rafael Martinez's teeth down his throat if he messes with my sister. Is that supportive enough for you?'

'Actually, I was thinking you should spend some time with them, and then you'd see that they actually love each other.'

The pilot's voice came over the intercom, smooth and clear. 'About to start the descent into Vienna.'

Relief touched Gabe's face—clearly this conversation wasn't something he felt comfortable with. Etta knew she should leave it—knew it was none of her business—but as she looked across at him she felt an urge to know why he was so resistant to closeness, what made him tick.

Stop, Etta. The old adage that curiosity killed the cat had some truth in it. Best she leave well alone and focus on Vienna and more immediate concerns. Such as how to face four days as Gabriel Derwent's Christmas girlfriend.

Yup, she must have been insane to agree to this—and yet as she gazed out the window of the jet anticipation swirled within the tumult of panic.

CHAPTER TWELVE

HOLY MOLY, MACARONI! Etta gazed round the suite, sure that her eyes must have bugged out. 'This is...' Words failed her.

The suite was even more impressive than the hotel's lobby—a vast, glittering golden parquet enclosure with stucco ceilings, enormous chandeliers and mirrored surfaces that refracted and shone.

But this... 'You could fit my entire apartment in here three times over.'

'Courtesy of April,' Gabe said. 'She pulled some strings and managed to get us this.'

'Why?'

'I don't know, but I have my suspicions. No doubt she'll have a source here keeping an eye on us.'

'Oh.'

Etta looked around the sumptuous room, decked out with renaissance lavishness. Gold curtains and tassels and brocade all combined to display elegance and luxury, and more chandeliers abounded. The panelled domed ceiling and intricate plaster cherubs spoke of the hotel's origin as a Viennese palace, but the main feature of the suite, seen through two enormous mirrored sliding doors, was the bed. Ornate and splendid, its carved headboard was a work of art in itself, and thick, sumptuous bejewelled curtains were draped around the super-king-sized bed.

Bed. In the singular. Yes, it was big enough to house a family, but it was still *one* bed.

As if he read her thoughts Gabe's lips upturned in a mixture of amusement and rue. 'We'll need to share it. If April has a source the last thing we want is a story questioning why one of us is sleeping on the sofa.'

He had a point, so she needed to focus on the size of the bed... No, she needed to forget about the bed. Because all of a sudden the memory of The Kiss fermented in her brain, her pulse racked up a notch, and her skin heated.

Wrenching her gaze from the four-poster, she headed towards the window and gave a cry of delight. 'Look, Gabe! It's snowing.'

The white flakes swirled down lazily and landed among the shimmer of Christmas lights and crowds of Christmas shoppers.

'It's beautiful,' she whispered, and turned to find him right behind her.

Her breath caught at his proximity and an insane yearning hit her for this to be real. For them truly to be here on a romantic getaway. For a moment the possibility hovered in her brain. Hadn't he said all those weeks ago that the ball was in her court?

No. Too dangerous, too risky, too much.

'So, what's the plan?' she asked.

'You tell me.'

'This is what Cathy and I usually do—we take it in turns to choose something. Write it down on pieces of paper, put them all in a hat and then take turns picking them out.'

Gabe blinked, and instantly Etta felt foolish. 'But obviously *we* don't have to do that. It's a tradition with me and Cathy, and this is my first holiday without her in sixteen years, so... Old habits die hard.'

'It's fine. Let's write some things down. The only thing I have already done is book tickets for a Christmas Eve concert at the Schönbrunn Palace.'

'That sounds magical. Which orchestra?'

His jaw tensed, but his voice was light as he named the ensemble.

'Oh, I'll research that...'

'It's two days away. How about we get on with this papers-in-a-hat thing? Have you even *got* a hat?'

'Of course I have a hat. It's December. I have a bobble hat! With a reindeer motif.'

Ten minutes later Etta pulled out a piece of paper with Gabe's scrawl on it.

'Shopping,' she read out. 'You want to go *shopping*?'

'I was being nice.'

'You mean you thought *I'd* want to go shopping? For what? I mean, I want to go to a Christmas market or two, but that's not what you meant, is it?'

'I assumed you'd want to hit the shops. My treat.'

'*Your* treat? Why?' Hurt strummed inside her. 'You've known me for weeks—you know that's not what I would do even if this were a real fling. Which obviously it's not going to be.'

Gabe ran a hand down his face. 'I guess I feel I owe you. I tricked you into a situation you didn't want to be in. I figure you may as well have some of the benefits. Seeing as you've chosen to pass on others.'

For a fraction of a second Gabe's gaze skittered towards the bed and Etta felt heat touch her cheeks. Without permission her imagination ran riot—if this were a real fling she was pretty sure they'd be spending most of their time in that very bed. As for shopping… She'd bet good money that lingerie was usually on his list.

The idea sent liquid heat to her tummy and she forced herself to hold her ground and his gaze. Prayed he couldn't read her thoughts. 'OK. Thank you. But how about you agree to being dragged around lots of museums instead? Although first you get to choose something you really want to do.'

'Anything?'

His gaze raked over her and Etta knew he'd made a pretty accurate perusal of her brain. Words failed her. Her mouth opened but no response would come out.

Eventually he took pity on her. 'Ice-skating sounds like a plan. Outdoors, cold, energetic… Sounds like what I need right now.'

Him and her both, but… 'I've never ice-skated before.' And the idea of making a fool of herself in front of Gabe didn't appeal.

'I'll teach you. It'll be fun.' His smile widened. 'Unless you're chicken, of course?'

'I'm not chicken. I'm *cautious*. My parents weren't very keen on risk, and since having Cathy neither am I. I've always been worried that if anything happened to me there would be no one to look after her.'

The words made her pause. They had been true enough when Cathy was small, but now… Now she felt a surge of irritation with herself. Was she really such a worrier that she wouldn't go ice-skating for fear of…*what*, exactly? How had that happened?

'Let's go.'

'Good girl. What's the worst that can happen?'

'I fall over and someone skates over my finger and—'

'I won't let that happen. Come on.'

They walked through the grandeur of the lobby and through the small revolving doors onto an illuminated street. The cold flakes of snow sizzled on Gabe's upturned face and next to him Etta gasped.

Above them hung shimmering sheets of sparkling lights that twinkled and twisted and glittered in a cascade of light. The shops were lit up too, literally wrapped in Christmas lights in the shape of a bow, and bedecked with silk ribbons and pine branches. The smell of roast chestnuts

mingled with the aroma of traditional *glühwein*—
a heady mix of wine, cinnamon and cloves.

'Incredible…' she breathed as they mingled with
the shoppers.

'So, Christmas market first, then ice-skating—
or the other way round?' He looked down at the
map.

'Market first,' she decided. 'Just in case I end
up in hospital.'

'Ye of little faith. I told you I'll keep you safe.'

'Martial arts expertise is *not* going to stop me
falling on my backside.'

'Ah, but my expert intuition will. OK, we'll do
the market first. We can easily walk to the one
outside the Hofburg Palace and then walk to the
rink.'

'Lead the way and I can look at all the lights.
Look! Each street is different. There must be literally millions of LED lights throughout this city.'

Etta was right—the brilliantly lit streets boasted
stars and garlands in a display that caught his
breath. But in truth it was Etta who affected his
lung capacity. Dressed in black jeans and a dark
green jumper with a snowflake motif, under a
brilliant red coat that emphasised her slender waist
before swirling out to knee level, she looked beautiful. Back in the hotel Gabe had wanted to pick

her up and kiss her senseless and he still wanted to do exactly that. But he wouldn't because it needed to be Etta's decision.

A ten-minute walk brought them to the immensity of the Hofburg Palace, its sandstone walls and green domed roof a mix of architectural styles— Gothic alongside Renaissance, with Baroque and Rococo thrown into the mix.

'It's a place full of history.' Etta's face lit up with enthusiasm. 'Though it's hard to believe that a family, even a ruling one like the Habsburgs, actually *lived* in something so enormous. It occupies fifty-nine acres and it's got 2600 rooms. Sorry. I am *so* boring to go on holiday with. I read up on everything and spout facts and...'

'It's fine. I'm interested.' His words were true, but more than that he was enjoying the way she waved her hands around to make a point, the enthusiasm on her face, her appreciation of the sights.

'Lucky for you. Because it's one of my hat choices. And I really want to visit the Sisi Museum—it's all about the Empress Elizabeth... Her life was fascinating and tragic.'

'It makes Derwent Manor look minuscule.'

Etta tipped her head to one side in consideration. 'I know it's very different, but have you ever considered the idea of handing the manor over to a heritage trust? You could still live in it, but the enormous upkeep costs wouldn't be borne by your family.'

'No!' The idea filled his Derwent soul with repugnance. 'Derwent Manor belongs to the Derwents. To hand it over to an institution would feel wrong—the land is our land, the rooms are ours, the history is ours.'

And yet thanks to him perhaps once he was gone the manor *would* be handed over, because the new Duke might not want to live in it. This Matteas Coleridge might not feel any loyalty to the property at all—why would he? *No.* Somehow, by hook or by crook, he'd imbue Coleridge with pride in his lineage. Bring him up to scratch.

'Derwent Manor will remain privately held.'

Etta's eyes scanned his face. 'OK. I just wondered if there isn't a part of you that resents the fact that you will have to live your life a certain way in the name of duty.'

'Nope. Not a particle.' It was hard to explain the deep tie he felt to his ancestral home, his abiding need to preserve it at any cost. And yet he'd let it down...

But right now he didn't want to think about his inability, his failure to his land and home. Didn't want to think about Matteas Coleridge—the man he was here to see. There was little he could do right now, and he wasn't even sure what he would achieve by an observation of the man who might one day wear the Fairfax coronet. Better to focus on Etta and her glowing features as she turned towards the market.

'I don't even know where to begin—and apparently this is one of the smaller markets. It's all so magically Christmassy.' Etta pulled her phone out of her coat pocket. 'I have to send some pictures to Cathy. Look at those Christmas decorations! They are exquisite.'

The hand-painted baubles hung in colourful array, glinting in the December sunshine. Next door to them was another pristine white stall where beautifully crafted reindeer jostled with snowflakes and the walls displayed intricately embroidered Christmas stockings. Brightly coloured shelves were decked with snowman figurines and snow globes.

'And the candles! They smell heavenly.' Etta darted from stall to stall, her enthusiasm evident in the way she gently touched the wares, considered her purchases. 'I know I won't see Cathy for Christmas, but I've promised her we'll have our own Christmas once…once we're settled.'

Her gaze challenged him but Gabe said nothing. Clearly Etta hadn't abandoned her run-from-Tommy idea, but Gabe let it go. Her explanation of her adoptive parents' behaviour, the information she'd shared about Tommy, had given him an understanding of her decision even if he didn't agree with it. Etta had had to face such a lot on her own.

His chest tightened at the thought of the sixteen-year-old Etta, terrified and alone. But from somewhere she had found the strength to escape Tommy once, with no help from the parents who should have supported her. Gabe knew his own parents would have been the same—their way or the highway. Well, Etta had chosen the highway and travelled that road to success—he couldn't blame her for running now.

'What do you think of this?'

She held up a chunk of soap for him to smell and her proximity sparked desire as he bent his head to inhale the sandalwood aroma.

'I like it,' he murmured, but as he straightened up his gaze rested on her face. 'Subtle, but tantalising. Spicy with a hint of sweetness.'

Her face flushed as awareness shimmered in the air—the same awareness that had glimmered into being the very first time they'd set eyes on each other. Only now it hummed with a deeper note, its pull stronger.

Etta blinked once, and then again, and shook her head slightly. 'Speaking of sweet...' She gestured to a bakery stall. 'Those smell divine. I need to try something but I can't decide what. There's gingerbread, and apparently that is a must, but I want something savoury too. Maybe a pretzel or...' She glanced at yet another stall and inhaled with appreciation as she read from the blackboard. '*Kartoffelpuffer*. They smell amazing. Shallow fried potato pancakes. Mmm... What do you think?'

'I think we should have both—savoury *and* sweet. We're on holiday, after all.'

'Sounds good to me. Let's eat.'

They walked through the rest of the market, both quiet now. The silence was comfortable, and yet Gabe noticed that Etta took care to keep her distance—presumably as aware as he that the slightest touch could cause them to combust. In truth he would welcome it—he wanted Etta, but only if she was fully comfortable with the idea.

'Ready to skate?'

Fifteen minutes later they had approached the outdoor rink.

Etta peered through the panelling. 'Look...' she breathed. Skaters of all ages, all shapes and sizes twirled and pirouetted in a display of expertise, to the strains of classical music that lilted from the outdoor speakers.

Ten minutes later Gabe and Etta approached the ice.

'So tell me—exactly *how* good are you at this and how much are you going to show me up?' she asked.

'I'm not an expert, but I can hold my own. I've played ice hockey before, so I'm more of an ice athlete than a dancer.'

'Hmm… OK. Let's give this if not a whirl then at least a wobble.'

Etta stepped onto the ice, pushed off with far more bravado than sense, and gave a yelp as she pitched forward. Without hesitation Gabe glided over and grabbed her round the waist, pulled her up, and held her steady.

The people around them receded and all there was was *this*. The feel of Etta in his arms…the warmth of her body against his…the smell of strawberry…the scratch of her bobble hat against his chin. She tried to move backwards, nearly lost her balance again, and clutched his arms.

A small gurgle of laughter escaped her lips. 'This is awkward.'

But it didn't feel awkward to him. 'It doesn't

have to be. All you have to do is hold on to me and you won't fall.'

Her eyes widened and for a long moment their gazes locked. He saw the uncertainty in her eyes, along with a flare of heat that flecked the tawny gold with amber.

'I… You… What is happening to me?' Her voice was low and vibrant with a hint of anguish.

'The same thing that is happening to me, and it's OK to feel it, Etta. There is nothing wrong with attraction.'

'I know that in theory—but I haven't felt like this in a long time, Gabe, and I'm not sure I like it.'

'I'm not Tommy. I would never hurt you.'

'I know that. I promise I do. But…'

'It's OK, Etta. I don't want you to feel pressured in any way at all. Whatever you decide to do with this attraction I'm good with it.' He smiled down at her.

Her laugh was shaky. 'That darned ball is still in my court?'

'Yes, it is.'

'Then let's skate.'

The snow had stopped and glints of late sunshine dappled the cold whiteness of the ice. Gabe's arm around her waist felt warm and right and it played havoc with her senses. The exhilaration of gliding on the smooth ice, the laughter in his voice as he instructed her, the passion in his eyes as they rested on her caught her breath in her throat, filled her with female joy.

Gabe wanted her and he was honest enough to admit it. Suddenly Etta was tired of the pretence. The attraction existed and it was impossible right now to regret it. It enveloped them in a mesh of anticipation, and each movement, each word was filled with innuendo and sensual overtones. Each touch sent her pulse a notch higher, brought another hint of desire into play.

Time seemed to float by as he instructed her, clasped her hands in his and skated backwards, towing her along. He encouraged her, teased her, praised her, and all the while his eyes conveyed a message of need and desire until her whole body was heightened to fever pitch, every sensation on alert.

A warning alarm tried to clang in her mind, telling her that this was too much, but as the crisp air nipped her cheeks, as the swirling snow fell in magical flakes around her and the Christmas music added cheer to the air, it was impossible to think that this could be wrong.

All her life she'd believed in what her parents had imbued her with—she was inherently flawed, programmed to do wrong, her natural instincts would lead her astray and into wrongdoing.

Tommy had proved them right—she'd entered into that relationship like a fool. But Gabe wasn't Tommy and she wasn't that teenage girl any more.

'I think you're ready to let go now,' Gabe said. 'Skate by yourself.'

Etta braced herself and pushed off and gave a small squeak of delight. 'I can do it!'

Exhilaration surged through her as she glided forward in a smooth movement, the classical music adding rhythm to her advance. Next to her Gabe grinned, and desire spiked inside her.

'This deserves a glass of Viennese punch. I'll meet you in the middle of the rink.'

As they made their way across the ice Etta knew what she wanted and exactly what to do about it.

If she had the guts.

Minutes later she held a steaming mug and sipped the sweet, hot brew—a mix of tea, sugar, rum and brandy.

The scent of cloves wafted upwards as Gabe lifted his mug. 'To new experiences.'

Etta nodded, and her stomach looped-the-loop as her nerves jostled and twanged. *Now or never.*

Balancing carefully, she placed her own mug down on the stand, took Gabe's from his grasp, and placed it next to hers. 'I can think of another new experience I'd like to try.'

With that she glided forward, reached up, and pressed her lips against his.

Sensations zapped her body in a warm molten stream as synapses pinged and went into overload. For the first time Etta knew what a timeless moment was. Her body moulded to his as his lips played feather-light havoc with her senses. Touched her own lips with a sweetness that morphed into an intense vortex as she parted her lips and he deepened the kiss. Her hands looped round his neck and his large hands spanned her waist and pulled her even closer to him.

When finally he ended the kiss he rocked back, though his hands still anchored her to his body. 'Any more new experiences you want to try?'

His deep tones danced over her skin and she released a sigh of sheer anticipation as she batted her eyelashes at him in exaggerated flirt mode. 'Hmm… Perhaps you could help me out?'

'Let's go.'

Her whole being was now consumed by a need he seemed to empathise with fully as they tugged their skates off, fingers made clumsy by haste. But eventually they entered the dusk of the Vienna evening. Snow whirled down once more, and Etta marvelled that it didn't sizzle as it landed on her heated face, on lips that tingled from sensory overload. The lights looked even more magical now, and she slowed her quick march for a few minutes to listen to the jaunty medieval carol being strummed by a busker with a harp outside the festively lit shops.

Back at the hotel, they crossed the lobby, went down the corridor and into the suite. The door closed behind them and she stepped forward, straight into his arms, lifting her face for his kiss.

But although he wrapped his arms around her waist, his eyes were serious as he looked into her face. 'Etta, are you sure about this?'

'Yes. I haven't felt like this in years, and I want this.'

Caution etched his forehead with a frown and she knew why.

'You once told me I was a fool to give up on sex, love, and companionship. Love and companionship aren't for me, but you've convinced me sex is worth a shot. I want to join the ranks of your liberated passionate women who can do a fling.' She wanted to know she wasn't still living her life as if her parents watched and waited for her to screw up. 'So...' She smiled up at him. 'What are you waiting for? The ball is in *your* court, Gabe Derwent.'

'Now, *that* isn't a problem at all.'

The smile that accompanied the honeyed words was downright sinful, and her skin shivered in response.

'Let's start like this...'

His hands dropped to the belt of her coat and he unbuckled it in one deft movement and shucked the woollen garment down over her shoulders.

'I think we can get rid of this too...'

Seconds later her jumper joined her coat in a colourful pool.

'Your turn.'

Without hesitation, her fingers trembling with unabashed greed, she slid her hands under the pure cotton of his top, heard his intake of breath as she touched his skin, ran her hands over his glorious chest.

'Come on.' In one clean movement he scooped

her into his arms. 'It would be a shame to waste that bed. Let's move this over there.'

A few strides later and he'd laid her on the decadent bed and was looking down at her, his eyes dark with raw desire.

She reached up and pulled him down next to her.

CHAPTER THIRTEEN

ETTA OPENED HER eyes and blinked as she absorbed the vast stuccoed ceiling, the deep gold of the folds of curtain that hung from the bedposts. Then the ornate splendour was obliterated by memories of the previous night and warmth swathed her body with a flush of remembered pleasure, joy and wonder tinged with a hint of anxiety.

What should she do now? What would one of Gabe's liberated women do?

Turning her head, she looked at Gabe—took in the strength of his bare chest, the sprawl of his long limbs tangled in the sinful silk of the sheet—and something tugged at her chest.

Whoa, Etta. Don't mix up the physical and the emotional. That way lay stupidity of Mount Everest proportions. What Gabe had given her last night was the realisation that she was capable of passion, of the giving and taking of pleasure, and for that she owed him a debt that she wouldn't fuzz with any other feelings.

He opened his eyes, went from drowsy to instant alert, and his lips curved up in a sinfully decadent smile. 'Morning, gorgeous.'

'Good morning.'

As if he sensed her hesitation he reached out. 'It is—and I know how to make it even better.'

His deep chocolate drawl with its wicked note of laughter dissolved the remnants of her reservations. 'Hmm...that sounds like a proposition I'm happy to explore.'

'Exploration was exactly what I had in mind.'

And then Etta got lost in the magic and the sizzle and the sheer exhilaration of the moment, until the dawn light had given way to bright Viennese winter sunshine that streamed through the gap in the brocade curtains.

Eventually... 'What shall we do today?' Gabe asked. 'I think we may need to add more options into the hat. But, whilst spending the whole day in bed has its plus points, I don't want you to miss out on Vienna. So over to you.'

The temptation to remain in bed was nigh on irresistible—but way too dangerous. She was Etta Mason, eminent historian, and she would not let herself forget that. Outside the hotel was a city that she had always wanted to visit, and she wouldn't be distracted from that.

Yet somehow her mood didn't lend itself to visiting a museum, or even the historic splendour of a palace. 'I'd like to go on the giant Ferris wheel. Apparently it's an experience not to be missed.'

'Leave it to me.'

By the time Etta emerged from the luxurious magnificence of a marble bathroom that was big enough to do the Viennese waltz in, complete with domed ceiling and chandelier, Gabe was standing at the window of the lounge, dressed in jeans and a thick knitted dark blue jumper.

'All sorted,' he said. 'Let's go.'

The sky was clear and their breath mingled white in the cold air as they stepped onto the busy Viennese streets, walked side by side, and Etta marvelled at the difference twenty-four hours could make. Now her awareness of Gabe had heightened into a knowledge of exactly what would happen if she succumbed to temptation, and the added frisson sent a small shiver through her.

As if still attuned to her body, he turned to look down at her—and there was that smile again... enough to bring heat to her face and a vague echo of her mother's disapproval. *No.* There was nothing wrong in what had happened last night and *zip* to be ashamed of.

They approached the amusement park and Etta tipped her face up to view the imposing, truly giant Ferris wheel silhouetted against the Viennese landscape. She absorbed the hustle and bustle of the fairground, the excited shrieks of kids and adults as they braved the roller coaster, the scents of pastries, schnitzel and hot dogs mingled into an evocative mixture.

'I've hired a private gondola,' Gabe said, '1897-style. Plus a champagne breakfast.'

'What a lovely idea. Thank you.'

Looking up, she smiled at him just as the click of a camera made her whirl round.

The man gave her a thumbs-up. 'Looking good, Gabe.'

A fleeting frown touched his face before the Derwent smile took its place. 'Now you've got your picture we'd appreciate some privacy.'

'No problem. As long as I get the heads-up on your dinner plans.'

'No deal—because we haven't decided as yet.'

The photographer discreetly moved away, presumably content with his picture, and Etta composed her features. 'So we have photographers following us around?'

'I figured it was better to arrange a photo opportunity—with any luck, that will be it for the day.'

'You told the photographer we'd be here?' It was
an effort to keep her voice light, to remind herself
that the reason she was here was to play the part
of Gabe's temporary girlfriend. It made sense that
he had given the photographer the information.

'Yes. I always figure it's better to have a good
relationship with the press—usually if I tip them
off they take a photo and then leave me alone. I
should have mentioned it.' He shrugged. 'I guess
I'm so used to the publicity I don't think about it.
Sorry, Etta.'

'It's not a problem.'

She was tempted to ask if he'd booked the Ferris
wheel ride for the benefit of the press coverage,
as proof of their relationship, but she pressed her
lips together and held the words at bay. It didn't
matter, because Gabe always saw the bigger picture and always liked to be the one who painted it.

'It is if you're upset.'

'An angle you didn't consider?' She'd meant to
utter the words lightly, but she recognised the note
of hurt. 'Sorry, Gabe, that came out wrong. I'm
not really a public person unless it's to do with
my job, but for the next few days this *is* my job.'
It was a reminder to herself as much as to him.

She grinned up at him suddenly. 'And I intend to enjoy it.'

'Good, because so do I.'

Etta followed Gabe to the front of the queue and soon they boarded a red gondola. The simple interior had wooden slatted walls, and light streamed in through the six windows to illuminate an elegant round table set for two. Champagne flutes glinted in the winter sunlight and silver cutlery gleamed next to pristine white napkins. The aroma of coffee tantalised, and an array of breakfast items topped the damask tablecloth— *semmeln*, pats of creamy butter, glass jars of apricot jam, ham and boiled eggs.

'This looks amazing. But I'm not sure we'll be able to eat it all on one rotation of the wheel.'

Gabe shook his head. 'Each rotation is about thirteen minutes. We get to stay on for six rotations, so we have plenty of time to eat and enjoy the view.'

His eyes rested on her as he said the last words and her tummy turned to mush.

'Shame there are so many windows so all I can do is look.'

Her legs threatened to turn jelly-like and she sat down as the wheel began to move slowly. Gabe seated himself opposite and poured her a glass of bubbly, followed by a glass of orange juice. 'Cheers.'

Etta clinked her glass against his and then sipped the golden liquid. 'This is madly decadent. Steph and Cathy would definitely approve.'

'How are they?' he asked.

'Loving the cruise. The Caribbean was an enormous hit, and Cathy says she wants to live in New York one day.'

'You must miss her.'

'Yes. But…'

But not as much as I'd expected. There came that familiar nudge of guilt-laced panic. Because, like it or not, she suspected the reason for that was sitting opposite her. *No need to panic.* Given the choice she'd be with Cathy for Christmas, and soon enough she *would* be with her daughter and they would embark on a new phase of their lives. Gabe would be a treasured but distant memory.

'But what?'

'But I need to get used to it.' Etta improvised with a different truth. 'Cathy is growing up, and it could be that she *does* decide to live abroad for a while, and that's how it should be. I don't ever want her not to do something because she's worried about me.'

'You're a great mum. You know that, right?'

Warmth touched her at the sincerity in his voice. 'I've done my best.'

'It can't always have been easy. Seventeen and on your own with a baby.'

'It *wasn't* easy.' There had been times when fear and panic and sheer exhaustion had threatened to overcome her. But through it all she had known she could never give up Cathy. She had wanted to give her baby everything her own parents—birth and adoptive—had failed to give Etta. 'But I wanted to give Cathy the best I could—both in terms of love *and* lifestyle.'

'You could be a role model for young single mothers. Or for teenagers who are having a rough time. You pulled yourself from a dark place. I know how much you could help some of the kids I work with—' A shade of annoyance crossed his face as he broke off.

'The kids you work with?' Kaitlin's words came back to her. *Has he told you about his charity work?*

Gabe hesitated, reached for a roll and buttered it, as if debating whether to close the conversation down.

Then he gave a lift of his broad shoulders. 'It's no big deal but it's not something I publicise. I work with a charity and I offer self-defence classes for kids who've been bullied or have suffered physical abuse. Sometimes the bullies come in as well. Often the reason they're bullying others is because they've been bullied or abused themselves—it's a vicious cycle that needs to be stopped. A lot of them come from difficult backgrounds and are in care, or they're on their own and isolated.'

'So how long have you done this charity work and how come you haven't publicised it? Surely that would be advantageous?'

'It's a personal thing.'

'Personal?' Etta surveyed him across the table as her mind pieced together various comments he'd made. She made a leap in the dark. 'Were you bullied at school?'

His body stilled and she was pretty sure it wasn't in reaction to the gentle lurch of the gondola as the wheel it made its way round.

'Yes. Again this isn't public knowledge, and I don't want it to become so. But I'd rather you knew the truth than speculated.'

Etta shook her head. 'I won't tell or speculate. But…that must have been hell. I…I guess I didn't think someone in your position would ever be bullied.'

'My boarding school was rife with bullying, and in fact I made the perfect target. The older boys decided I was stuck-up and needed to be taken down a peg or two.'

His voice was matter-of-fact, but Etta's heart twisted at the image of an eight-year-old Gabe, his blue-grey eyes filled with fear, being hurt.

'It was a long time ago, Etta.'

Maybe, but she was pretty damn sure he still carried the scars. 'How long did it go on for?'

'Until I got old enough and skilled enough to stand up to them.'

'But that must have been *years*. Why didn't you tell anyone? Your parents? A teacher?'

'Telling a teacher would have made it worse—the teachers wouldn't have been able to protect me twenty-four-seven. Plus, that would have been snitching.'

'What about your parents?'

No answer. And as Etta studied his expression she suddenly knew with utter certainty that he had told his parents and they had done nothing.

'As I said, it was a long time ago. I dealt with it, I learnt from it, and now I'd rather not talk about it.' He made a gesture to the window. 'We're nearly at the top.'

Conversation closed.

Reaching across the table, she covered his hand, hoping her touch conveyed sympathy and admiration as she gazed out at the panoramic view of Vienna. Her breath caught in her lungs, but Etta was unsure whether it was due to the incredible landscape from two hundred feet up or the feeling of warmth that Gabe had confided as much as he had—trusted her with such personal information.

'It's amazing.'

Equally as amazing were the next two days that soared by.

Minutes spun into hours, time cascaded in a fairy-tale warp and Etta lost herself in an exquisite maelstrom of sensation with every sense heightened.

The sights of Vienna were bright and vivid, with the boldness of modern art displayed in opulent baroque backgrounds. The smells and tastes of schnitzel, *glühwein* and *apfel strudel* and the dark richness of coffee lingered on her tastebuds.

And throughout it all there was Gabe. His lightest touch caused her entire body to hum with desire and the nights were filled with the touch of silken sheets, his warmth and strength, his gentleness and laughter and the intensity of shared passion.

Until somehow Christmas Eve arrived, and

from the moment they woke Etta sensed Gabe's withdrawal.

There was no laughter or teasing, no fleeting touches that spoke of intimacy. It was nothing she could encapsulate in words, but it was in the tension of his shoulders, the clenching of his jaw, the distance he kept between them as they walked to the Schönbrunn Palace for the concert.

'So we tour the palace and then go to the Orangery for the concert?' Etta knew the answer, but for the first time in days the silence between them was laced with awkwardness.

'Yes.' Gabe had his hands deep in the pockets of a grey overcoat that topped a charcoal suit. As if aware of the brevity of his reply, he added, 'The tour is guided and people are split into groups of ten.'

'It should be great. The Orangery is meant to be magnificent. It was built in 1754 by Franz I and it's very baroque. Joseph II used to have banquets there, with illuminations in the citrus trees, and Mozart conducted his singspiel *The Impresario* there in 1786—'

Etta broke off. Why on earth was she trying to fill the silence by spouting like a tour guide? Perhaps to counter the clench of misery in her tummy. It was an irrational sadness. Was this the etiquette of a fling? To start to pull back as the end approached? Maybe it was a strategy she should emulate—after all, once Christmas was over it would be time to get on with her real life. This was an interlude, with no more bearing on reality than the fairytale it was. Only this fairy tale didn't end in happy-ever-after. It ended with no strings attached, never to see each other ever again.

But no matter. Right now there was Christmas Eve to be enjoyed, in this incredible setting that would stun any fairy-tale princess, and she would make the most of it.

The palace was lit up, shining in all its splendour, and the Christmas market outside was a hive of bustle and cheer. The enormous Christmas tree was simply decorated with white lights and overlooked a life-size hand-carved nativity scene that imbued Etta with a sense of awe.

But as their tour of the palace commenced for once Etta couldn't find it in her to marvel at the Imperial splendour. Even as she gazed on the most magnificent of ceiling frescoes, the grandeur of the white-and-gold rococo decorations, and the incredible crystal mirrors that created a near magical illusion of blurred other dimensions, her entire awareness was focused on Gabe.

Her antennae registered his tension, growing like a fast unfurling plant, until finally she said, 'Gabe, is something wrong?'

CHAPTER FOURTEEN

GABE FORCED HIS body into a more relaxed stance—not an easy task when every muscle seemed filled with tension, every sinew torqued with strain.

Pull it together and answer the question.

He smiled down at Etta's concerned expression. 'No. Nothing is wrong.'

Except for the fact that in mere minutes he would see the man who might one day bear the title that Gabe had believed would pass to his own child. It wasn't a big deal—dammit, he was *glad* Matteas Coleridge existed, relieved that there was a possible alternative heir so the title would not die out. Yet right now anger and bleakness pulsed inside him because fate had decreed that he couldn't have children.

Enough. Whingeing at the unfairness of life was pointless and ineffective.

'I'm fine.'

'Are you sure? You seem different, somehow.'

'Not me.' Gabe dug deep and discovered the famous Derwent charm, the smile, the expression. But Etta's frown only deepened. 'You're imagining it.'

Turning from the searching look in her tawny eyes, he studied the blue and white porcelain on display and tried to quell his sense of impending doom.

Tour over, they completed the two-minute walk to the Orangery. Once inside, he waited until Etta had settled herself onto a comfortable seat below the glittering extravaganza of the chandelier and seated himself beside her. The orchestra, dressed in eighteenth-century costume, were already assembled, and Gabe's heart pounded his ribcage as his eyes scoured each member.

There he was. Gabe rested his gaze on a stocky, brown-haired man, cello in hand, his eyes closed as if in inner preparation for performance. Visceral pain sucker-punched Gabe so hard he expelled a breath, and Etta turned to look at him.

With immense effort Gabe leant back in the chair and forced his voice into action. 'It should start any minute.'

To his relief, before Etta could respond the conductor rose to his feet and started to speak. Minutes later music swelled around them. The classical pieces fluted and strummed through the air, mingled with motes of history, and it was almost possible to imagine that Mozart himself stood on the stage.

But somehow for Gabe each and every glorious note evoked images of the children he'd once thought to have, and grief and loss for a now impossible future swirled in his gut.

On some level Gabe registered the next couple of hours. The choice of pieces was a perfect mixture of the haunting and the lively, and the conductor was both knowledgeable and witty. When a pair of ballerinas came onto the stage they were greeted with a universal murmur of appreciation, and after their performance applause rang out. Next up was an opera singer, whose voice soared and dipped with notes so pure and melodic that Etta gasped next to him.

Yet throughout, his whole being was attuned to Matteas Coleridge, his body feeling cold and hot in turn, taut with the fight-or-flight instinct.

At one point he became aware of Etta's glance and then her hand reached out and covered his. *Damn.* No doubt she'd sensed his discomfort, and for a moment he wanted to accept the unspoken comfort she offered. *No.* That way lay weakness; he would not allow any closeness with Etta other than their physical connection.

He had to pull himself together and man up, and so gently he pulled his hand away. Forced his emotions into shutdown, made himself focus on Matteas Coleridge with calm. Then he turned to Etta with a smile, refusing to acknowledge the hurt in her brown eyes.

'The finale should be magnificent,' he murmured. Almost as if he were speaking to a chance acquaintance.

In truth the finale was more than magnificent—the Viennese orchestra played in complete harmony, with an intensity that left their audience spellbound and captivated, and when the last strains of the music graced the high-vaulted room there was a moment of silence before a standing ovation.

But even the beauty of the music couldn't permeate the ice he'd generated around his emotions, and Gabe was glad of it.

'Back to the hotel for a late supper?' he suggested.

'Sure.' Etta looked up at him, her eyes narrowed slightly. 'I just want to pick up a programme on the way out. It'll make a great souvenir.'

Gabe considered a protest, then decided against it. Etta might well simply buy the programme and not study it in detail. So he merely nodded, waited whilst she purchased the glossy bound booklet, and then they set off through the Viennese streets back to the hotel.

Gabe knew he should try and manufacture some sort of conversation but somehow it seemed beyond him—perhaps once they were back at the hotel, surrounded by the chatter and bonhomie of their fellow guests, it would become easier. But he did derive some strange solace from Etta's presence as she walked beside him, their steps in time as they passed the still brightly lit shopfronts, and after ten minutes they reached the now familiar environs of the hotel.

'Can we pop upstairs quickly before we eat?' Etta asked.

'Sure.'

Once in their suite Etta vanished into the bedroom, sliding the door shut behind her. Gabe walked to the window and looked out into the Viennese night. Matteas Coleridge existed; he'd seen him in the flesh and his mission to Vienna had been accomplished. No, not fully. It was Christmas tomorrow, and he wanted the day to be special for Etta—however unfestive he felt himself. Then, after Christmas, he would go home and face the music.

Gabe frowned, wondering what Etta was doing.

It was unlike her to change for a meal—especially as she had looked pretty smokin' in the green dress she'd worn to the concert.

As if on cue the door slid open and Etta stepped forward, halted on the threshold of the palatial lounge area. Foreboding issued him with a qualm. She hadn't changed—stood tall in the simple green dress, which was given a twist by the fall of its asymmetric hem which emphasised the length of her legs. She had the concert programme folded open in one hand, and as he met her tawny gaze he flinched inwardly at the hurt that lurked behind anger.

Gabe steeled himself—he'd known this was a possibility and he had a strategy in place.

'Why didn't you tell me?'

'Tell you what?'

'That "Matt Coleridge", a cello player in that Viennese orchestra, is Matteas Coleridge, your newly discovered distant cousin.'

'I didn't think it was important.'

Disdain narrowed her eyes. 'That doesn't fly, Gabe. You must have known I'd be interested. Is that why we're in Vienna?'

'In part. I was curious. And when I found out he was in that Viennese orchestra I figured, why not? I wanted to get away for Christmas so why not Vienna?'

Nice and casual. No big deal.

But Etta wasn't buying it—that much was clear from the frown on her face and the twist of her lips.

'But you didn't want anyone else to know? Not your sister, not April, not anyone?'

'No. Poor bloke—I wouldn't want to unleash April onto him just because I wanted to satisfy a curious impulse. As for Kaitlin… She has enough on her plate.'

'You don't get curious impulses.' Etta's voice was tight. 'If you don't want to tell me what's going on, fine, but don't insult my intelligence. You didn't want anyone to even *know* you'd commissioned the new family tree. Why not?'

'That's my business. I hired you to do a job—you did it and you've been paid. Subject closed.' A small voice told him that this was the wrong approach. A louder voice informed him that he was being a complete arse.

'No.' Etta strode forward, her pleated skirt swirling in the angry movement. 'The subject is *not* closed. I don't understand what's going on, but I know I've been manipulated. You hired me as your cover—your fake girlfriend. What happened?' Her voice broke and she gave an angry shake of her head in denial. 'Is that what all this has been about? You and me? An additional cover to make it real for April's spy, so no one suspects why you're really here?'

The revulsion in her tone was directed in equal measure against him *and* herself.

'That is not true.' He didn't want her to believe that—not when he knew what a leap of faith it had been for her to trust her feelings, trust her physical instinct. 'I wouldn't use you.'

Disbelief gazed back at him from her eyes. 'But that is *exactly* what you've done. You used my professional expertise and then you used me. This whole fling has been an illusion, created to throw dust in everyone's eyes for reasons of your own—a master strategy.'

Damn it. He couldn't let her believe that, but the alternative…the alternative was to trust her. She had already worked out some of the facts…could already do damage.

As if she could read his thoughts she gave a small scornful laugh, devoid of all mirth. 'Don't worry, Gabe. I won't go blabbing your secret to April or to anyone else. We had a deal and I'll keep my part—I'll even keep up the fake girlfriend charade for the next couple of days.'

She rubbed her hands up and down her arms, and for a second she looked lost.

'But I don't care who April's spy is—we aren't sharing that bed. And I will be out of here on the first available flight on Boxing Day.'

Let it be.

That always worked. Only it didn't. He couldn't let Etta believe he'd used her, that the past days had been fake, an illusion.

'I can't have children.'

The words reverberated, caromed off the patterned wallpaper and lingered in the air, each syllable a portent of fate. The act of saying the words out loud banded his chest with harsh reality, and his lips twisted in a grimace as he took in her expression.

Etta's mouth opened and closed, and shock etched each delicate feature even as her tawny eyes filled with compassion and near-empathy. His gaze twisted from hers. He didn't want her pity—couldn't bear to see her commiseration.

'Gabe...'

The programme fell from her grasp, swished to the floor, and as if the soft thud had galvanised her she closed the gap between them. She reached up and cupped his jaw in her palms, angled his head so their gazes locked.

'Look at me. I'm *sorry*. More sorry than words can express.'

The sincerity of her voice and the feather-lightness of her touch mingled and grief threatened to surface. Gabe shoved it down—no way would he give in to misery.

'It's OK. You don't need to say anything.' Gently he lifted his hands and removed hers, squeezed gently and then let go and stepped back. 'I've had a while to come to terms with it.'

'How long have you known?'

'Nine months. Since then I've seen three separate experts—top men and women in their field. I've looked into treatment options, but I am one of those rare cases for which they don't believe treatment will result in success.'

The bitter tang of disbelief was still there—he'd been so sure he could fix the problem.

'So the unbroken father-to-son Fairfax line will be broken. But what worried me most was the idea that the title might die out altogether. Thanks to the convolutions of the law and the way the Fairfax peerage was originally set up the title can't be passed on via a female. So any children Kaitlin and Cora have can't succeed.'

'So that's why you hired me?'

'Yes. I needed you to find out if there was anyone out there to suceed me. You found him—Matteas Coleridge. The possible one day Duke of Fairfax.' Try as he might, he couldn't keep the acid note from his tone. *Stupid.* He had *wanted* another heir to be found, for Pete's sake. This way there was a chance for the future. 'Potential founder of a new dynasty.'

The words made her flinch. 'Gabe. This sucks. You must be devastated. Why didn't you tell me?'

'Because no one knows. I wasn't sure how the news would affect my father's health. I was worried it would tip him into another attack.'

'So is that why you split with Lady Isobel?'

'Yes. Isobel and I have always known our parents wanted us to marry—we talked about it when we were young and we agreed it suited us both. She wasn't interested in love any more than I am—she wanted a title, the position of duchess, to be the mother of a future duke. She was very clear that she wants children, so I figured it was probably worth making sure I could back up what I had on the table. When I found out the truth I knew we couldn't go ahead and get engaged as planned. But I still thought there must be a fix—a treatment of some sort. So I told Isobel I needed to postpone the engagement and I took off for America, because I figured it would be easier to avoid publicity there whilst I got the problem sorted.'

'But Isobel must have been curious?'

'Isobel didn't seem to mind—after all, what difference would a month make?'

'So what happened?'

Gabe shrugged. 'You've got me there. I have no idea. Next thing I knew she gave that press conference without any warning at all—the one that denounced me as a heartbreaker. I called her and she said she was sorry but she didn't want to get married any more, and she'd figured the best way to get herself out of it was to stage that interview.'

Etta looked at him with narrowed eyes. 'Why didn't you expose her?'

'Because there was no point. I hadn't been totally up-front with her, she would no longer want to be my a wife, so why stand in her way? There was nothing in it for me. And it meant I didn't have to tell her the truth.'

'So what will you do now?'

'Explain the situation to my parents. Following Dad's heart attack my parents are understandably keen for me to marry and produce the next Derwent heir. They need to know that although I can't do that there is another possibility—that way the family can take Matteas in, groom him… Could be my parents will ask me to abdicate my position so they can take him in hand.'

The whole thought made the blood turn to ice in his veins but it was an option that had to be considered. Now that he had seen Matteas in the flesh he knew it to be a feasible reality.

'No. They wouldn't—they couldn't do that.'

'If he's the right type of guy they could do *exactly* that. If they think it is better for Derwent Manor, for the future of the title of Duke of Fairfax, of course they will.'

'And will you agree?'

'Possibly.' Though every emotion revolted, he knew that in reality he would have no choice. 'If I agree that it's best for Derwent.'

'But what about what is the best option for *you*?' Etta's voice was gentle. 'What about you, full-stop? All you seem to care about is the effect on Derwent. You must be devastated on a personal level about not having children. Have you taken the chance to grieve for yourself?'

'Grief won't provide a solution. One way or another Matteas Coleridge might.'

It almost helped to speak the words out loud as he paced the carpeted floor.

'Option one: I remain in line for the title, marry a suitable duchess, look after the estate and imbue

Matteas and his family with centuries of heritage. Or I stand aside now and he takes my place when my father dies. It depends on Matteas.'

'No, it doesn't. It depends on *you*. In any case, your parents will *want* you to succeed them. You are their *son*. They *love* you.'

Gabe shook his head, touched by her misplaced certainty. 'The Derwents don't work like that. Love isn't in the Derwent vocabulary. My parents will transfer their loyalty to Matteas if they believe he is a worthy heir.'

'That *has* to bother you.'

'They believe the future of Derwent is more important than all the emotions and dramas of today.'

'But it still must hurt to believe your parents could transfer their feelings so easily. I *know* it does, so don't try and con me into believing you aren't feeling *something*.'

'There is no point in giving in to feelings.'

'Maybe. But those feelings exist, however much you suppress them. If you don't want to talk about it I truly get it.' Etta hauled in a breath, met his gaze square-on. 'I was fourteen when my mum fell pregnant with Rosa. When she was born I worked out that something wasn't right... There were questions Mum couldn't answer, or the answers she gave didn't ring true. Also they were different with Rosa than they were with me—tactile, demonstrative, loving, *happy*. They adored her—truly adored her—and it was as if I didn't exist any more. They wouldn't even let me help look after her.'

Gabe could see the remembered hurt and bewilderment on her face and he stepped towards her. This time it was her turn to step back, with a small shake of her head.

'The point is I eventually worked it out—I'm adopted, but they hadn't ever told me. I asked them and they admitted it. Like it wasn't a big deal. But it was—one minute I had an identity, and the next, *kaboom*, the whole facade tumbled down, leaving *me* as the debris.'

Gabe knew how that hurt—the collapse of a lifetime's belief—and the pain on her face caused his chest to tighten as he imagined a teenage Etta, caught in a maelstrom of pain and confusion, hurt and anger. So much made sense now—her fear of losing Cathy's love, her belief that Cathy would transfer her love to Tommy.

'Etta, I'm sorry.'

'That's not why I told you. I told you because you're treating something devastating as something logical, and it isn't. You thought you had a future and now that future has been snatched away from you. Well, I thought I had a past and that was ripped away from *me*. And it sucks. This I know.'

Warmth touched him that she had shared something so personal, so distressing, in order to help him, and for an instant he almost felt an urge to allow the emotions he'd leashed so tight for months to run loose. But that would mean letting Etta closer, and he'd let her close enough. Anything further would smack of weakness—but he was in control and he would find a strategy to move forward.

'Come here. I appreciate what you have told me, and I promise you that it outweighs anything I'm going through. I will deal with my parents—however it pans out, and whatever goes down. But right now there is one thing I need you to know.'

He stepped forward, cupped her jaw in his hands, and tilted her face towards his.

'I *didn't* use you in the past few days. I *didn't* sleep with you to pull the wool over April's eyes. I slept with you because I wanted to.' He smiled, wanting—*needing*—to change the mood. 'I still do. And it's important to me that you believe that.'

She surveyed him, her brown eyes soft with emotion. 'I do. I do believe that—and thank you for telling me the truth. I promise you can trust me, and if you want to talk—not about strategies and logic but about how you *feel*—I'm here.'

'Thank you.'

That would happen when hell froze over—he wouldn't know where to begin, even if he had any desire to invite Etta to a pity party.

'In the meantime, let's skip supper and go to bed.'

CHAPTER FIFTEEN

GABE ENTERED THE bedroom where Etta still slept, curled on her side. One hand pillowed her cheek and she looked so beautiful his heartstrings tugged.

She opened her eyes and surveyed him drowsily before she rolled onto her back and then pushed herself up against the ornate splendour of the headboard.

'Merry Christmas,' he said, surprised to feel anticipation unfurling in his gut as she grinned at him.

'Merry Christmas!' A stretch and she inhaled appreciatively. 'What *is* that heavenly smell?'

'Rise and shine.' He tugged at the duvet and she snatched at it. 'I ordered Room Service. Pancakes, Viennese-style. I know it's not the same as having Cathy here, but I thought it might help to have your traditional breakfast.'

Her smile illuminated the whole room and made him feel about eight feet tall.

'Thank you, Gabe. I'll be out in two minutes.'

'Take your time—and wish Cathy a merry Christmas from me.'

True to her word, minutes later she sat opposite Gabe and looked at her heaped plate. 'Wow!' The thick golden pancakes had been torn into bite-sized pieces, sugar-dusted and piled into an artistic tower. Berries bedecked the concoction and gave the dish a festive edge.

He wiggled his eyebrows. 'I thought you might be hungry after last night.'

'You thought right.'

She dug into the pancakes and nearly moaned at the light texture, at the taste of custard and sugar melting on her tongue.

'These are *amazing*. But now it's your turn for a present.'

Sudden discomfort made him shift on the brocade chair. 'You didn't need to…'

'I wanted to. It's Christmas.'

One more spoonful and then she rose and went over to the cabinet, returning with a beautifully quilted deep red stocking, embroidered with an image of Father Christmas—presumably purchased from one of Vienna's numerous Christmas markets.

'Here you are. Happy Christmas. I'm sorry if

it's a bit over the top. I thought that because you said your parents didn't do stockings…'

'Thank you.' There was a small awkward moment. 'Really. I'm not sure what to say. The Derwents aren't very experienced in receiving presents. But I really mean the thank you.'

'The best way forward is to open them.'

Her small chuckle, the eager expression on her face, suddenly made it easy to smile and Gabe grinned at her.

'Here goes!'

He delved a hand in and tugged out his gifts. First a bottle of Viennese wine, then sandalwood soap, a snow globe, and chocolates.

'Etta, thank you. I'll always remember my very first stocking.'

For a millisecond a cloud hovered: the realisation that it would in all likelihood be his last, that he wouldn't ever hang up a stocking for his own children.

As if she'd read his thoughts she reached out and quickly touched his arm, before reseating herself opposite him. 'I know you will have thought about this, but not being able to have birth children doesn't mean you have to give up on having a family. You can adopt.'

'No, I can't. Adopted children are prohibited

from inheriting a title or the land. I won't bring up a son on Derwent Manor and then tell him he can't inherit because he's adopted. It wouldn't be fair. As for adopting a daughter... It wouldn't feel right to deliberately adopt a girl just because she couldn't inherit anyway.'

'I truly believe if you tell the truth from the start it wouldn't be a problem. If my parents had done that I think it would have made a monumental difference to our relationship. For them *and* me.'

'I won't take that risk. I know what it feels like to face the prospect of watching another man take over the land I have learnt to love.' It was exactly the scenario Gabe now faced. 'The Derwents have to have children to further the Derwent line.'

'I don't believe that. Surely you want children for yourself? Because you want to be a dad?' Etta frowned. 'Is it that you don't want to adopt because you don't want any children who don't carry your blood?'

'No. It is truly the children I am thinking about.' His lips straightened into a grim line. 'If I inherit the title I can't adopt. If I stand aside I won't marry at all. My "shallow playboy life" can continue apace. But let's not talk about this—it's Christmas, after all.'

For a moment he thought she'd pursue the topic, but then she nodded. 'OK.'

'Good. I've got a gift for you as well.'

Etta's face creased into puzzled lines as she accepted the small wrapped piece of card and opened it. '"Max Woodstock, Martial Arts Master",' she read out.

'I want you and Cathy to go and get some lessons. I want to know you can defend yourself. Max is the best. I've spoken to him and he'll teach you himself. Lifetime of free lessons.'

'Thank you.'

Etta rose and came round the table, wrapped her arms round him. The unfamiliarity of being hugged caused him to tense for a moment, and then he followed suit, inhaled her vanilla scent as her hair tickled his nose.

'That's incredibly thoughtful.'

'Knowing martial arts makes you walk taller, with more confidence, and you'd be surprised how far that alone goes in getting people to back off.' People such as Tommy. 'Now, let's go and enjoy a Viennese Christmas.'

'Maybe we could go to the service at the cathedral?' Etta suggested. 'I know it's not the same as a country church, but it would at least be one of your traditions.'

So they strolled the illuminated Viennese streets, called out greetings to strangers, all smiling and full of festive cheer. Horse-drawn carriages clip-clopped down the road, the horses' breath showing in clouds in the crisp December air. They stopped to join a cheery crowd that surrounded an outdoor piano-player whose fingers flew over the keys with breathtaking skill.

Then there was the cathedral, dominating the skyline with its four towers and famed roof tiles in a colourful zig-zag pattern that depicted the coat of arms of the Austrian Empire. Gargoyles spouted water in figurative defence of demons, and the Gothic portals displayed a wealth of detail that had absorbed Etta's attention for nigh on an hour on their previous visit as she'd examined the biblical scenes, beautifully portrayed with glorious symbolism, alongside the more macabre winged sirens, entwined dragons and two dogs with a single shared head.

In truth, Gabe had been more captivated by her absorption than by the undoubted craftsmanship. He'd studied the focus in her brown eyes, the curl of her chestnut hair against the delicate nape of her neck, her grace as she'd hunkered down to examine a detail more closely.

The interior of the cathedral was filled with

people, a mixture of those there for the Christmas service, and tourists enthralled by the statues, frescoes, and paintings. The ambience was weighted with history, and above them the immensity of the arched ceiling inspired awe.

It was an awe that resounded throughout the beauty of the service—in the language that rolled out from the ornamental pulpit and the sound of the choir soaring and swooping in choral harmony, touching the air with a feeling of universal peace and goodwill.

Once it was over they mingled with the crowds and headed to the entrance, though Etta lingered to study the thoughtful figure of St Augustine with a book, mitre and an inkwell, leant down to peek at the self-portrait of an unknown sculptor under the steps.

'I want a last look. That's the trouble—there is so much in the world to see, but I fall for places and I want to come back.'

'Like the café?'

The one Etta had fallen for on day one and insisted on returning to.

'Exactly like the café. I'm a creature of habit.' Her smile was rueful. 'So can we go back there today? I checked and it's open on Christmas Day.'

They entered the café, a historic haven, chocka-block with tradition and frequented by philosophers and royalty over the years. High vaulted ceilings, painted archways and splendidly covered seats sprinkled with damask cushions gave the coffee house a regal glory. Notes tinkled from the piano as jacketed waiters glided over the floors with silver trays held aloft with stately expertise.

'I can't believe I can be hungry after that breakfast, but I am. I'll have the Viennese potato soup with mushrooms followed by a piece of *sachertorte.*'

This brought a smile to his face—Etta had also completely fallen for the torte that Vienna was famed for—especially the café's speciality: a dense chocolate cake with thin layers of jam.

The rest of the day passed by in a magical Viennese swirl.

They walked the gardens of the Schönbrunn Palace, then returned to the hotel and luxuriated in the depths of the black marble bath, complete with Christmas bubbles scented with marzipan. Then their dinner was brought and served by a butler so stately that Gabe blinked.

'He looks more dukelike than *me,*' he said as the man made his dignified exit, and Etta gurgled with laughter.

Conversation flowed—easy talk, with both of

them skirting any conversation that would remind them this was the end. Course followed course. Pheasant, goose ravioli, boiled beef and then gingerbread mousse. Each and every dish complemented the one before, and when it was over they stood by the window and gazed out over the still busy streets, illuminated in gold and white.

'Happy Christmas, Etta.'

'Happy Christmas, Gabe.'

As he took her hand to lead her to the bedroom it occurred to him that it *had* been. It had been the interlude he'd needed before harsh reality set in.

But now he needed to face his parents and set about carving out a new life.

Etta shifted on the bed, fought the idea of waking. She wanted to stay asleep, meshed in drowsiness, her mind and body still ensconced in the memories that fizzed and bubbled. The night had been magical—a magic wrought of Christmas and happiness, passion and sweetness and love.

Her eyes sprang wide in shock... *Love?*

Oh, no. No, no, no, *no*. Etta forced herself to remain still, to keep her breathing even as panic threatened to engulf her. This could *not* have happened.

It dawned on her that a noise had awoken her—

it was still pitch-dark outside but a faint buzz provided a welcome distraction from the enormity of her stupidity. Until her brain and her ears connected. *Oh, God.* Was it her phone? Where *was* her phone? The phone she faithfully placed next to her bed every night. In case Cathy needed her.

Panic swarmed her brain cells as she scrabbled on top of a gold leaf cabinet. *Not there.* Scrambling out of bed, she tried to think... It must still be in her bag, probably nearly out of charge...

She ran into the enormous lounge, tried to recall where she'd dropped her bag, found it on the sofa and fumbled the phone to her ear.

'Cathy? Are you OK?'

'I'm fine, Mum. Actually I was worried about *you.* But I've just realised the time—did I wake you up? Sorry... I miscalculated the difference. We tried you twice yesterday. I wanted to tell you about...'

Etta sat perched on the chaise longue, listening to the babble of her daughter's conversation, and relief washed over her. Cathy was safe. But what if she hadn't been? What if she had been trying to get hold of her and it had been an emergency? What if the unthinkable had happened and Tommy had tracked her down? What if Cathy had needed her?

Guilt slammed into her, caught her breath.

'Mum? You sure you're OK? Your Christmas sounded pretty good… What's the plan now? Is the fake-girlfriend gig over?'

'Yes.' Etta forced brightness into her voice. 'It's over. I'll be flying out of Vienna today. I'll be in England when you get back, and we'll work out where to meet.'

She couldn't risk going home yet—there had been no sign of Tommy in Vienna, but there had been enough publicity that he would know exactly where she was.

Cathy's sigh carried down the phone and across the miles with gale force. 'Mum. *Please.* Let's drop the cloak-and-dagger stuff. We've already missed Christmas together. Let me meet Dad, let him into my life, and it will all be fine.'

The words sounded so reasonable but Etta knew she was wrong. 'I can't do that, Cathy. Your dad is dangerous and abusive.'

There came the memory of pain, physical and mental, of the sensation of worthlessness, the belief that she deserved to be hurt, the twisted certainty that Tommy loved her—*would* love her if she could only be less useless. She could not let Cathy be sucked into that vortex in her need for a father. A need *she* understood all too well.

'So the "cloak-and-dagger stuff" continues. In the meantime enjoy the rest of the cruise and I'll call you later.'

'Fine.' Cathy gusted out another tornadic sigh.

'I *do* get how you feel, Cathy, and I love you lots.'

'Love you too, Mum.'

Etta disconnected and tried to think—she was an idiot, a fool, a disaster zone. Once again she'd allowed herself to get sucked in. Gabe might not be Tommy, but that wasn't the point. The problem here was Etta—*she* couldn't handle relationships of any sort—not even a fling. Instead she flew out of control, lost perspective. Last time the cost had been her self-respect and her family. This time she might have lost her daughter.

'Stupid, stupid, *stupid.*'

'Who's stupid?'

Etta started and looked up to see Gabe standing between the open mirrored doors that separated the living room and the bedroom. Instant reaction shook her.

Get it together.

No matter what happened, Gabe must not suspect she'd fallen for him—*stupid* didn't even touch the sides of her folly.

Say something. Anything.

'Cathy. That was Cathy. She still wants to see Tommy. Which is pretty stupid. But really I meant myself. I haven't exactly come up with a plan.'

Slow down, Etta.

She sounded deranged—like Daffy Duck on helium.

'Let her see him. Once.'

'We've been through this. I will *not* take that risk.'

'She loves you, Etta. Her loyalty is with *you*. Give her a chance to prove that. She'll see through Tommy.'

'You don't know what it's like to want a dad— to fantasise about the perfect man who will turn up and look after you. I *do* know.'

Somehow it seemed important that before she left, Gabe should know everything. She wanted him to understand, not to judge her and find her wanting. It shouldn't matter to her, but it did.

'I was a doorstep baby. My birth parents left me on the doorstep of a church in Henrietta Street. That's where my name came from. The authorities tried to trace my parents but they never came forward. I've tried to trace them too, but I haven't managed it. I have fantasised about their identity for years, and if someone turned up claiming to be my dad I'd believe whatever he said, whoever he was. Cathy will be the same.'

There was silence as he absorbed her words. Then he stepped forward and tugged her into a hug, and for a treacherous second she rested her head on the breadth of his chest and drew solace from his strength.

'That's tough. You must have so many questions.'

Stepping back, she knew with crystal-clear certainty that it was the last time he would hold her, and she could feel the crack appear in her heart. The pain made her catch her breath.

'I do. But I accept now that they won't ever be answered. My parents—my adoptive ones, I mean—assumed the worst. That my birth parents were drug addicts who simply didn't care about me. I think that's why they had trouble bonding with me. They were desperate for a child, and they convinced themselves and the social workers that it would all work out, but it didn't. They tried to *pretend* I was their child, but the whole time they were watching me, waiting for my blood to out itself. They tried to love me, but when Rosa came along they had an instant bond—they loved her without effort. I guess that didn't happen with my birth parents and me.'

Sadness touched her—what had been so wrong with her that they hadn't left her any clue as to her identity?

'You don't know that. They may have left you because there was no alternative.'

'Maybe. The point is, whether that's true or not, if they had turned up when I was a teenager and claimed to be saints I would have believed them— no questions asked. Cathy will be the same about Tommy.'

'No. Because Cathy has *you*. You had no one— you have always had to face things alone. Your adoptive parents weren't there for you when you needed them most. *Hell*. They weren't there for you at all. Little wonder you dreamt about your birth parents being perfect. Cathy won't do that. Trust yourself, Etta.'

His voice was deep with sincerity, but how could she trust herself when she'd blithely fallen in love with Gabe? A man who wanted a suitable aristocratic wife or a playboy lifestyle…a man who eschewed love and closeness.

She got *why*—Gabe had been packed off to boarding school, abandoned to the bullies, and expected to work it out for himself. He'd been brought up without love and believed that to show love was to show weakness. And Gabe wasn't a weak man. He was a man bound by duty and choice to follow a certain path in life. A path he couldn't share with Etta even if she wanted that. And she didn't—wouldn't risk what love did to her. How it messed with her head. She was safer, happier alone.

Yet misery weighted her very soul at the idea that she would never see him again. Never touch him, laugh with him, or wake up cocooned in his arms. If she didn't leave now she'd cave, throw herself at him, and in the process lose all self-respect.

What was *wrong* with her? Her relationship with Cathy was forged in bonds of steel and love—how could she have let herself be distracted from that? For a man who didn't want her? Her lungs constricted and a band of grief tightened her chest. She *had* to get out of here.

'I need to go. Thank you for everything.'

Gabe's forehead was etched with a deep frown. 'Whoa. Not so fast.'

Gabe tried to force misplaced panic down. 'What's going on, Etta? I thought your plan was to leave tomorrow.'

Think, Gabe.

But for once his brain refused to cooperate.

Strands of thought whirled and swirled and he couldn't correlate them, couldn't formulate a strategy.

Part of his mind was still trying to assimilate the extent of what Etta had faced in her life. To learn that she had been abandoned by her birth parents at the same time as learning she was adopted and then being rejected by her adopted parents… Little wonder she'd rebelled in a bid to win her parents' attention. But the consequence had been a plunge into an abusive relationship and a teen pregnancy.

Admiration seethed inside him as he looked at her, standing amidst the imperial grandeur. Yet for once he couldn't read her emotion—her expressive face was in shut-down, though she still rubbed her hands up and down her arms.

'It was, but I've changed the plan. I need to get to Cathy. Christmas is over and I need to be with my daughter. I need to talk to Steph and work out our next step. I need to get back to my real life. This week has been magical, and I'll never forget it, but it wasn't real. It was a fling—an interlude.'

Her lips turned up in a smile that didn't get anywhere near her eyes.

'Fun, with no strings attached, and now I need to move on.'

Strange how his own words seemed so hollow now. Panic rocked him back on his heels as he realised that he didn't want her to leave. *Insane.* What did he want? Another day? Another week? What difference would that make? He didn't know, but he knew he couldn't let her leave yet, had to make sure she was safe.

'We both need to move on,' he managed, the words redolent with strain. He forced his vocal cords into submission. 'But we need to make sure we do this right. We'll fly back to London together and go to a hotel. Then we can smuggle you out.'

'I may go and stay in Cornwall at the Cavershams' Castle Hotel. I can hole up there and—'

'Ethan could collect Cathy from the cruise ship and bring her to you.'

Ethan would protect Etta and Cathy, and that was the most important issue at stake.

'I can work out our next move from there. I'll start packing.'

There it was again—that near desperate urge to stop her, to take her into his arms and tell her he would keep her safe from Tommy, hold her close. But along with that came the surge of panic, the memory that closeness led to weakness, made you vulnerable to pain and loss and fear. If you let people close, you opened the door to pain. He'd nearly slipped up with Etta. Somehow she'd slipped under his guard and under his skin and he needed to get her out.

The best way to do that was to shut down all emotion.

This had to end now.

Yet he could sense the bleakness seeping in under his armour, trying to touch his soul.

CHAPTER SIXTEEN

Two weeks later

GABE LOOKED ROUND the lounge at Derwent Manor and wished he could shake the memories of Etta—it was absurd to wonder if he could smell a hint of vanilla in the air.

His parents glared at him across the room.

'What *is* going on, Gabriel?' His father's tone was testy, at best. 'You should be out there securing Lady Isobel Petersen.'

'Your father is right.' The Duchess's tone was glacial. 'Plus you shouldn't have asked Kaitlin to come. And, Kaitlin, you shouldn't have come—what will Prince Frederick think? It's his mother's birthday banquet and...'

For a moment Kaitlin looked as though she might respond with an unheard-of suggestion as to what Prince Frederick could do with the banquet, but instead she smiled her trademark smile.

'I'm sorry, Mother, but Frederick understands

that my brother has to come first. I know Gabe wouldn't have asked us all here on a whim.'

Baulked, the Duchess turned to easier prey. 'As for summoning Cora...' Her green eyes stared down the table at the younger of her twins with disdain.

Cora grinned back cheerfully, clearly unfazed, and Gabe blinked. Marriage had morphed his diffident sister into a confident young woman, no longer cowed by her parents. *Marriage or love?* a small voice asked him as he recalled Etta's insistence that it was the latter.

'Don't worry, Mother. Rafael and I aren't staying here—we've booked into a hotel nearby so you won't need to see him.'

Gabe had little doubt that Rafael Martinez would rather eat dirt than stay with his in-laws, and he couldn't blame him.

'So, Gabe, why *have* you summoned us to this family conclave?'

His heart hammered in his ribcage. This was the moment of truth—the point in time when this nightmare would become completely real. Hope tugged at his heart as he looked at the aquiline features of his father and his mother's serene beauty. The same hope he'd felt all those years ago when he'd run away from school. That they would show empathy, understanding… Even then he'd known that love was too high an expectation.

Gabe closed his eyes briefly, braced himself, unclenched his jaw. 'I can't have children.'

The room rang, echoed with absolute silence. His parents' expressions morphed from disbelief to disdain and Gabe's heart plummeted in his chest. Disappointment and near revulsion twisted the Duchess's mouth into a grimace of distaste. As for his father—his blue-grey eyes were colder than the Arctic at its worst. He was looking at his son as if he could not believe that a Derwent could have let him down on so spectacular a scale.

Then Kaitlin spoke. 'Gabe, I am so sorry.'

As if her sister's voice had broken the spell Cora jumped up, moved around the table to his side, and pulled him into a hug. For a second he resisted, and then he hugged her back, before looking towards his parents.

'I know it's a shock—'

'A *shock*? It's a disgrace.' The Duke banged his stick on the floor. 'A let-down.'

'It's not Gabe's fault,' Cora said quietly.

'Fault is irrelevant,' the Duchess said. 'We need

the next heir and now our son is unable to provide him.'

The look she gave Gabe was equivalent to one she might give to an experiment that hadn't worked to plan. Pain twisted his gut, but he refused to show it—after all, he had toughened up Derwent-style, and he would be damned if he'd let his parents see that their attitude hurt. He understood—always had understood—that the title, the land, the manor, and the Derwent name came first.

Yet in that instant his brain reeled as realisation socked him—that whole creed was *wrong*. Etta would *never* make Cathy feel like this—would be constitutionally incapable of it. He could almost hear her voice, knew exactly what she would say. *Nothing is worth more than your child's worth—their happiness and well-being is paramount.* Etta had lived her life by that principle and that made her truly wonderful. That was one of the reasons he loved her—she lived by her beliefs, had done so in the toughest conditions and won through.

What? Love?

That was preposterous. But true. The sheer incredibility of the knowledge, the strange joy that swirled inside him alongside panic threw his thoughts into turmoil.

Not now, Gabe.

'Actually, I have located the next heir. Matteas Coleridge. Late twenties, seems decent, lives abroad.'

'Never heard of him. Never heard the name.' The Duchess shook her head. 'How *can* you have let this happen?' For the first time there was a crack in her voice, as if the truth were sinking in. 'A line unbroken for centuries. And now, thanks to you...'

Cora spun round. 'How about thanks to Gabe for finding this other heir. I bet it wasn't straightforward. Plus, has it occurred to you how Gabe might be feeling? That he may be sad? Upset? Grieving? For himself? In his own right?'

'Cora. It's OK.' Gabe reached out and took his sister's hand. 'But thank you for the support. Truly, little sis.'

The Duchess turned a basilisk look on Cora. 'You always *were* vulgar, Cora. Marriage to a Martinez hasn't changed that.'

She rose to her feet and the Duke followed suit.

'We need to meet this Matteas Coleridge. Make it happen. If he is malleable and we deem it best you must step aside, Gabe.'

'*Excuse* me?' This time it was Kaitlin. 'You can't do that to Gabe. That's inhuman—and it's not your decision.'

'Enough.' Gabe kept his voice low but authoritative. 'This has been a shock. There is no need to make a decision yet. When it is the right time *I* will decide what I'll do.'

The Duke opened his mouth, but before he could speak Gabe rose to his feet.

'I think it's best if Dad gets some rest.'

The Duchess glanced at her husband's expression and gave a curt nod.

Once their parents had left the room Cora shook her head. 'They are *unbelievable*. But, Gabe, why didn't you tell us?'

'Because that's not what the Derwents do,' Kaitlin said as she leant forward in her chair, tucked a strand of red-gold hair behind her ear. 'But right now you need to tell us what we can do to help.'

'I don't think you can do anything, but I appreciate it that you want to.'

Kaitlin looked thoughtful. 'Was it Etta who found this Matteas Coleridge?'

'Yes.'

'Does she know the truth?'

'Yes.'

His sisters exchanged a glance.

'Do you love her?' Cora asked.

Yes, I do.

It explained so much. In the past two weeks there hadn't been a minute when Etta hadn't been in his thoughts. Everything brought back a memory of her—the smell of vanilla, the taste of venison, the sight of a woman with chestnut hair. Each thing made his heart ache because he missed her—missed her touch, the tilt of her chin, her smile, her chuckle, her courage. He missed Etta. Full-stop. Wanted her beside him, wanted to hold her, to protect her and...

And *enough*. How did this make sense?

Love made you vulnerable, opened up the route to pain and hurt.

But it also made you a better person.

Gabe knew he would do anything for Etta, and that if it cost him pain and hurt then that would be an acceptable price.

Only it didn't have to be like that. Being with Etta made him...*happy*. Her courage, her strength, her decision to take a leap of faith and have a fling with him, her vulnerability, her zest for life, her amazing ability to parent...

'Yes. I love her.'

Cora and Kaitlin looked at him.

'So what are you going to do about it?' Cora asked.

Two days later...

Gabe approached Etta's London address, crunched over the white layer of snow, smelt the tang of more snow in the imminent future. His nerves were stretched tauter than the proverbial tight-rope as he mounted the stairs outside Etta's apartment block.

Easy does it.

Could be Etta wasn't even there. His conversation with Ruby Caversham had simply unearthed the fact that Etta was still in London.

He buzzed the intercom of her flat and waited.

'Hello?'

Relief at the sound of Etta's voice dropped his shoulders. 'Hi. It's me. Gabe. Derwent,' he added. 'Can I come in?'

There was a pause and he wondered if she would refuse. Then, 'Of course.'

The formality of her tone was not what he wanted to hear, but at least she was letting him in.

The intercom buzzed again and Gabe pushed the

slightly dilapidated front door open and bounded up the stairs before Etta could change her mind.

Etta pulled the door open and led the way into a hallway separated from the rest of the flat by a closed door, painted a cheerful yellow. The hallway itself was an off-white colour that combined with the large mirror on one wall to give the tiny area an effect of space—a space well utilised with a coat and shoe rack.

She pushed the interconnecting door open to step into a small but welcoming lounge and headed to a spot behind a red sofa, her arms folded with more than a touch of wariness.

'Hey…' he said, his throat suddenly parched as he gazed at her.

Come on, Gabe.

He could do better than that. Only right now he couldn't—her beauty had caught his breath. Dressed in jeans and a dark red top, with her sleeves pushed up, chestnut hair pulled back with two clips he'd swear she must have borrowed from Cathy, she looked gorgeous.

'Why are you here, Gabe?' A small shake of her head. 'Sorry. That was rude. Would you like tea or coffee?'

He followed her gaze to the small kitchenette in the corner of the room, where again there was a feeling of cheer generated by the way Etta had combined clutter with clever use of space. Pots and pans hung from a handy contraption to the left of the sink. An array of fun mugs hung on hooks. A cork board was littered with notes and memos. The sofa held a collection of cushions, presumably collected from various holidays, and stacked tables made the small area feel like home.

'I'm fine.'

'OK.'

Another silence and he realised he was procrastinating because of fear—pure and simple. Time to get on with it.

'How have you been?'

'Good. You?'

'Yup. Good. Where's Cathy?'

'Sleepover at Martha's.'

'So how come you're still in London?'

Etta took in an audible breath. 'I was going to get in touch with you. I was just waiting until…' Her voice trailed off. 'That doesn't matter. You're here now. I did what you suggested. I put my trust in my bond with Cathy and I let her meet her dad. She loathed him.'

There was a wonder in her voice, along with pride.

'Apparently he turned on the charm and at first

it worked. Then he had a go at me and Cathy went nuts in my defence. He unravelled after that. Cathy says her curiosity is satisfied and she never wants to see him again. He was so angry he went out, got drunk, ended up assaulting someone, and is now back behind bars. I know he'll always be a danger, but both Cathy and I will keep seeing Max for martial arts training, and we've decided to live our lives. So thank you—you showed me that I could face up to Tommy and, most important, trust Cathy. That means the world to me.'

Pride and admiration filled him that Etta had been so brave, along with a feeling of satisfaction that she now knew and believed in her bond with Cathy and could lead her life untainted by fear.

'Don't thank me. *You* did it—you were the one brave enough to carry it through.'

'What about you? Your turn. Have you told your family about Matteas?' Her voice was brittle, her arms still folded.

'Yes. My parents do think I should consider standing aside if he comes up to scratch.'

'What do *you* think?'

'I'm not sure. That's why I'm here. I was hoping for your input.'

Etta's forehead creased in puzzlement.

'But I wondered if you'd mind coming back to Derwent Manor to discuss it.'

Gabe held his breath, the weight of hope that she would agree heavy in his chest.

'Now?'

'Yes. I'll drive you back later.'

Etta hesitated, and then nodded. 'Give me a minute to check in with Cathy.'

Ten minutes later Etta locked her apartment door, her mind whirring with an entire gamut of conflicting emotions, overridden by the megabuck question: what was Gabe doing here?

No big deal, Etta.

Gabe needed advice from one of the only people who knew the true facts. So she needed to focus on practicalities, not on the immense joy that wanted to surface at the sight of him. No way could she allow herself to reach out and touch him to check that he wasn't a hallucination from her dreams.

Yet she couldn't help but cast surreptitious glances across the car. Her body and mind absorbed his presence, stored the sight of his face, his blond hair, the depth of his blue-grey eyes, and the breadth of his shoulders into the Gabe Derwent treasure trove of her memories.

The drive to Derwent Manor was achieved in near silence as he concentrated on negotiating the roads through the snow that still cascaded down in lazy white flakes. Once they arrived Gabe drove past the imposing walls of the manor and parked outside a dilapidated old building.

Gabe unclipped his seatbelt. 'What do you think?'

Etta studied the house—it was old, and in need of repair, but in her mind's eye she cleaned and plastered the walls, replaced the cracked panes of glass, resurrected the roof, and tended the neglected lawn.

'It has potential.'

'That's what I thought.'

He smiled at her then—a smile so full of warmth that her toes curled in her boots and the yearning to wrap her arms around the breadth of his chest had her scrambling to get out of the car.

'Could I have a closer look?'

'Sure, but first I want to show you something.'

Etta followed Gabe towards a small glade at the edge of the building and halted at the scene before her.

The spruce trees were alight with the twinkle of lights—a magical glitter that evoked memories of the first time she'd met Gabe at the Cavershams'

Castle Hotel. In the middle of the wooded area a picnic table held a crystal vase overflowing with a burst of colourful flowers. The snow had slowed now, but still fluttered in lazy flakes to create a tableau that took her breath away.

Emotions jostled inside her: hope, perplexity, and wariness all attempted supremacy.

'Here.'

Gabe reached into the crook of the tree and produced a box, opened it and handed her a gold-wrapped package. Etta let out a soft sigh as his hand brushed hers and hurriedly attempted to disguise it with a cough.

'Open it.'

Etta complied, her fingers shaking as she gently tore off the embossed paper and opened the dark blue cardboard box inside. She lifted out an exquisite snow globe.

'Oh…'

Slowly she turned it in the dusky air and felt tears prickle her eyelids. Inside the globe were memories of Vienna—a miniature Ferris wheel, a Christmas tree, the palace, and a pair of ice-skaters. She shook it gently, watched the flakes swirl inside even as she tasted the cold tang of real snow on her tongue.

'It's beautiful. I'll treasure it and the memories always.'

'I wanted to say thank you.'

'For what?'

'For being you. And for showing me something precious.'

His voice was serious, yet with an overtone of warm chocolate that shivered over her skin. 'I don't understand.'

'You showed me the power of unconditional love. I thought everything in life was a barter, an agreement. You don't live *your* life like that. Your love for Cathy is and always has been without condition. From the minute she was conceived through to now. My parents don't work like that. We—Kaitlin, Cora, and me—we have always had to *earn* their approval. You arc always there for Cathy, to help and support her regardless. You were there for *me* without any request for yourself. You went the extra mile at the fair—even bought champagne and cooked to celebrate its success. You gave up your own Christmas for Cathy's safety, but without martyrdom. Instead you made Christmas special for *me*, gave me a stocking.'

'You made Christmas special for me as well,' Etta pointed out.

Gabe shook his head. 'As part of a deal.'

'No.' Etta shook her head. 'There was no need to order pancakes, or set me up for a lifetime of self-defence. There was no reporter there to record *those* things. You didn't *have* to try and convince me to face up to Tommy, to trust Cathy. You're a good man, Gabe. I know that.'

'Thank you.' Gabe hauled in a breath and gestured to the snow globe that she still held clasped in her hands. 'There's a compartment at the bottom. Open it.'

Etta did so and her mouth formed an O of disbelief as she saw the contents—an exquisitely delicate, multi-faceted diamond solitaire ring shone up at her. Her whole body stilled…her heart skipped a beat, somersaulted, and then pounded her ribcage as she tried to think.

Gabe stepped forward and picked up the ring. 'Etta. Will you marry me?'

'I…I…'

Yes, her brain screamed, *just say yes.* But she couldn't—not until she knew he was sure.

'But…I'm not suitable duchess material. I have nothing to offer on that score. And I don't want a marriage alliance based on what we bring to the table.'

Gabe visibly winced, then lifted one of her

hands and held it against his chest. She felt the pounding of his heartbeat against her palm.

'I love you, Etta. With all my heart. That's what I am bringing to the table. All I have to offer is my love. All I want is the chance to try and win yours. I love everything about you. Your generosity, your loyalty and your beauty, your courage. I love it that you're funny and that you love traditions and spout facts and embrace routine. And, most important, when you're not with me I feel like there's a piece of me missing.'

Etta's head whirled at the sincerity on his face, at the genuine timbre of his deep voice, at the way his gaze held hers, blue-grey eyes alight with a flare she knew was the real McCoy.

'I love you and I want to spend the rest of my life with you. No one else. I know you need independence, but I can eat cereal in my PJs whenever you want. I also know that I need and I want to get to know Cathy better, and if you give me a smidgeon of hope I know I can make you love me.'

For heaven's sake, say something, Etta.

But emotions tied her tongue—sheer happiness jostled with a need to reassure him, to... 'Gabe, I love you more than I can possibly tell you.'

'You do?'

'I do.' She stepped forward, straight into his

arms, and the feeling was so right her heart ached with happiness. 'I should have told you in Vienna but I panicked. I thought loving you would make me lose control and perspective, but it didn't. You helped me…showed me things about myself I didn't know. You made me believe in myself, trust in myself. You've shown me that love can be a wonderful thing, that we can be partners, make decisions together as a team. No one has to be in control.'

'So you'll marry me?'

'*Yes*. With all my heart.'

As he pulled her into his arms her head whirled with sheer joy.

'I love you, Etta, with my heart, body, mind, and soul.'

And as he slipped the ring onto her finger Etta knew that this was the best merger she could have ever made—an alliance based on love.

EPILOGUE

ETTA LOOKED AT her assortment of bridesmaids, all standing in the beautiful churchyard. The spring day was chilly but bright, and the sun glinted down from the cloudless sky.

'You all look stunning.'

The words were the absolute truth. Steph, Kaitlin, Cora, Cathy, and Martha all wore simple floaty chiffon dresses, short at the front and long at the back. Their outfits were fun yet elegant. Each was in a different shade—Cora in bold red, Kaitlin in teal-green, whilst Steph had opted for navy blue, and Cathy and Martha had decided on burnt orange and lemony yellow.

'Not as gorgeous as you, Mum,' Cathy said. 'But we *do* all look pretty fabulous. This wedding is going to rock.'

'Yes, it is,' Cora said. 'And, truly, you look beyond beautiful.'

For an instant nerves ricocheted through Etta even as she reminded herself of her joy in her dress—traditional ivory tulle with crystallised lace and gorgeous satin buttons and a chapel-length train. In a moment she would step forward into the historic church, which was bedecked with gloriosa and hyacinths and filled to the brim with aristocracy, celebrities, and royalty. All there to watch Etta Mason get married.

The realisation chased away her nerves. Because the press coverage, the many people she didn't know, the fact that she was on show, even the dress—none of it mattered. All that mattered was the fact that she would be walking down the aisle to Gabe, the man she loved with all her heart.

And there were some people who *did* matter in there. Such as her sister, Rosa, and her adoptive parents, to whom she had sent an invitation and who had agreed to attend. It was a first step, and Etta hoped it was a step towards reconciliation. Matteas Coleridge was also in attendance, in his new position as future heir. Because Gabe had decided *not* to step aside; he wanted to fulfil his role as Duke, not because of the kudos of dukedom but because he genuinely loved the manor and the Derwent lands.

Etta respected that, and she would stand by his side and support and help him as he would support and help her. As for children—that was something they would work out as they went along… the rights and wrongs of adoption…but Etta knew with bone-deep certainty that they would work it out together.

She took a deep breath and nodded at the women who surrounded her, and then she commenced her walk down the aisle. She had decided that she didn't want anyone to give her away. She was giving herself to Gabe, with a heart full of love and happiness. As she walked towards him and saw his awe-filled smile, his blue-grey eyes full of love, she looked forward to their future with joyful anticipation.

* * * * *

MILLS & BOON®
Large Print – March 2017

Di Sione's Virgin Mistress
Sharon Kendrick

Snowbound with His Innocent Temptation
Cathy Williams

The Italian's Christmas Child
Lynne Graham

A Diamond for Del Rio's Housekeeper
Susan Stephens

Claiming His Christmas Consequence
Michelle Smart

One Night with Gael
Maya Blake

Married for the Italian's Heir
Rachael Thomas

Christmas Baby for the Princess
Barbara Wallace

Greek Tycoon's Mistletoe Proposal
Kandy Shepherd

The Billionaire's Prize
Rebecca Winters

The Earl's Snow-Kissed Proposal
Nina Milne

MILLS & BOON®
Large Print – April 2017

A Di Sione for the Greek's Pleasure
Kate Hewitt

The Prince's Pregnant Mistress
Maisey Yates

The Greek's Christmas Bride
Lynne Graham

The Guardian's Virgin Ward
Caitlin Crews

A Royal Vow of Convenience
Sharon Kendrick

The Desert King's Secret Heir
Annie West

Married for the Sheikh's Duty
Tara Pammi

Winter Wedding for the Prince
Barbara Wallace

Christmas in the Boss's Castle
Scarlet Wilson

Her Festive Doorstep Baby
Kate Hardy

Holiday with the Mystery Italian
Ellie Darkins

MILLS & BOON®

Why shop at millsandboon.co.uk?

Each year, thousands of romance readers find their perfect read at millsandboon.co.uk. That's because we're passionate about bringing you the very best romantic fiction. Here are some of the advantages of shopping at www.millsandboon.co.uk:

* **Get new books first**—you'll be able to buy your favourite books one month before they hit the shops

* **Get exclusive discounts**—you'll also be able to buy our specially created monthly collections, with up to 50% off the RRP

* **Find your favourite authors**—latest news, interviews and new releases for all your favourite authors and series on our website, plus ideas for what to try next

* **Join in**—once you've bought your favourite books, don't forget to register with us to rate, review and join in the discussions

Visit **www.millsandboon.co.uk**
for all this and more today!